HOME

Praise for Kris Bryant

Lucky

"The characters—both main and secondary, including the furry ones—are wonderful (I loved coming across Piper and Shaylie from *Falling*), there's just the right amount of angst, and the sexy scenes are really hot. It's Kris Bryant, you guys, no surprise there."
—*Jude in the Stars*

"This book has everything you need for a sweet romance. The main characters are beautiful and easy to fall in love with, even with their little quirks and flaws. The settings (Vail and Denver, Colorado) are perfect for the story, and the romance itself is satisfying, with just enough angst to make the book interesting…This is the perfect novel to read on a warm, lazy summer day, and I recommend it to all romance lovers."—*Rainbow Reflections*

Temptation

"This book has a great first line. I was hooked from the start. There was so much to like about this story, though. The interactions. The tension. The jealousy. I liked how Cassie falls for Brooke's son before she ever falls for Brooke. I love a good forbidden love story."—*Bookvark*

"This book is an emotional roller coaster that you're going to get swept away in. Let it happen…just bring the tissues and the vino and enjoy the ride."—*Les Rêveur*

"People who have read Ms. Bryant's erotica novella *Shameless* under the pseudonym of Brit Ryder know that this author can write intimacy well. This is more a romance than erotica, but the sex scenes are as varied and hot."—*LezReviewBooks*

Tinsel

"This story was the perfect length for this cute romance. What made this especially endearing were the relationships Jess has with her best friend, Mo, and her mother. You cannot go wrong by purchasing this cute little nugget. A really sweet romance with a cat playing cupid."—*Bookvark*

Falling

"This is a story you don't want to pass on. A fabulous read that you will have a hard time putting down. Maybe don't read it as you board your plane though. This is an easy 5 stars!"—*Romantic Reader Blog*

"Bryant delivers a story that is equal parts touching, compassionate, and uplifting."—*Lesbian Review*

"This was a nice, romantic read. There is enough romantic tension to keep the plot moving, and I enjoyed the supporting characters' and their romance as much as the main plot."—*Kissing Backwards*

Goldie Winner *Listen*

"Ms. Bryant describes this soundscape with some exquisite metaphors, it's true what they say that music is everywhere. The whole book is beautifully written and makes the reader's heart to go out with people suffering from anxiety or any sort of mental health issue."—*Lez Review Books*

"I was absolutely captivated by this book from start to finish. The two leads were adorable and I really connected with them and rooted for them...This is one of the best books I've read recently—I cannot praise it enough!"—*Melina Bickard, Librarian, Waterloo Library (UK)*

"The main character's anxiety issues were well written and the romance is sweet and leaves you with a warm feeling at the end. Highly recommended reading."—*Kat Adams, Bookseller (QBD Books, Australia)*

"This book floored me. I've read it three times since the book appeared on my Kindle...I just love it so much. I'm actually sitting here wondering how I'm going to convey my sheer awe factor but I will try my best. Kris Bryant won Les Rêveur book of the year 2018 and seriously this is a contender for 2019."—*Les Rêveur*

Against All Odds

"*Against All Odds* by Kris Bryant, Maggie Cummings, and M. Ullrich is an emotional and captivating story about being able to face a tragedy head-on and move on with your life, learning to appreciate the simple things we take for granted and finding love where you least expect it."—*Lesbian Review*

"I started reading the book trying to dissect the writing and ended up forgetting all about the fact that three people were involved in writing it because the story just grabbed me by the ears and dragged me along for the ride...[A] really great romantic suspense that manages both parts of the equation perfectly. This is a book you won't be able to put down."—*C-Spot Reviews*

Lammy Finalist *Jolt*

Jolt "is a magnificent love story. Two women hurt by their previous lovers and each in their own way trying to make sense out of life and times. When they meet at a gay- and lesbian-friendly summer camp, they both feel as if lightning has struck. This is so beautifully involving, I have already reread it twice. Amazing!"—*Rainbow Book Reviews*

Goldie Winner *Breakthrough*

"Looking for a fun and funny light read with hella cute animal antics and a smoking hot butch ranger? Look no further...In this well-written first-person narrative, Kris Bryant's characters are well developed, and their push/pull romance hits all the right beats, making it a delightful read just in time for beach reading."—*Writing While Distracted*

"It's hilariously funny, romantic, and oh so sexy...But it is the romance between Kennedy and Brynn that stole my heart. The passion and emotion in the love scenes surpassed anything Kris Bryant has written before. I loved it."—*Kitty Kat's Book Review Blog*

"Kris Bryant has written several enjoyable contemporary romances, and *Breakthrough* is no exception. It's interesting and clearly well-researched, giving us information about Alaska and issues like poaching and conservation in a way that's engaging and never comes across as an info dump. She also delivers her best character work to date, going deeper with Kennedy and Brynn than we've seen in previous stories. If you're a fan of Kris Bryant, you won't want to miss this book, and if you're a fan of romance in general, you'll want to pick it up, too."—*Lambda Literary*

Forget Me Not

"Told in the first person, from Grace's point of view, we are privy to Grace's inner musings and her vulnerabilities...Bryant crafts clever wording to infuse Grace with a sharp-witted personality, which clearly covers her insecurities...This story is filled with loving familial interactions, caring friends, romantic interludes, and tantalizing sex scenes. The dialogue, both among the characters and within Grace's head, is refreshing, original, and sometimes comical. *Forget Me Not* is a fresh perspective on a romantic theme, and an entertaining read."—*Lambda Literary Review*

Whirlwind Romance

"Ms. Bryant's descriptions were written with such passion and colorful detail that you could feel the tension and the excitement along with the characters."—*Inked Rainbow Reviews*

Taste

"*Taste* is a student/teacher romance set in a culinary school. If the premise makes you wonder whether this book will make you want to eat something tasty, the answer is: yes."—*The Lesbian Review*

Touch

"The sexual chemistry in this book is off the hook. Kris Bryant writes my favorite sex scenes in lesbian romantic fiction."—*Les Rêveur*

By the Author

Jolt

Whirlwind Romance

Just Say Yes: The Proposal

Taste

Forget Me Not

Touch

Breakthrough

Shameless
(writing as Brit Ryder)

Against All Odds
(with Maggie Cummings and M. Ullrich)

Listen

Falling

Tinsel

Temptation

Lucky

Home

Visit us at www.boldstrokesbooks.com

HOME

by
Kris Bryant

2020

HOME

ISBN 13: 978-1-63555-853-1

This Trade Paperback Original Is Published By
Bold Strokes Books, Inc.
P.O. Box 249
Valley Falls, NY 12185

First Edition: October 2020

Credits
Editors: Ashley Tillman and Shelley Thrasher
Production Design: Stacia Seaman
Cover Design by Deb B.

Acknowledgments

This started off as a cute little holiday novella (like *Tinsel*) but grew into a short book. A big thank you to Sandy and BSB for moving things around to fit it in this year. I wasn't expecting the novella to keep going, but my characters weren't done telling me their story.

I had a ton of fun discussing this with my editor, Ashley. We pushed each other out of our comfort zones with this book. Hopefully, what we came up with is successful. Apparently, it's all about the gravy. Thank you, Shelley, for racing behind me picking up my grammar mistakes. There aren't enough red pens in the world, huh? Deb came up with the perfect cover, and honestly, I can't make my mind up if I love the dog or the woman more.

To my friends, thank you for encouraging me through a difficult year. A support system is so important when the world and life look bleak, but you ALL were there for me. 2020 didn't turn out the way we expected, but I can't tell you how much I appreciate you in my life.

And thank you, readers, for always picking up my books and enjoying my stories. Without you, I wouldn't be writing.

I know I say this a lot in my acknowledgments, but anything you can do to help our animal shelters is so important. Trust me, if I could be a professional dog cuddler, I would. There isn't a dog out there I don't try to turn into my best friend. My success rate is 99.7%. If you can't rescue a pet, consider donating pet food, blankets, towels, newspapers, money, or your time. You'll feel better about yourself. Animals rely on us. They can't tell us what's wrong or what happened to them. We can only trust our hearts and love them as much as they love us. Be a hero or heroine to fur babies everywhere.

To Molly
Thank you for finding your new home with me

CHAPTER ONE

Natalie pulled up the collar of her coat and crossed her arms to ward off the late-October chill that crept inside the sleeves and around her neck. This was her least favorite time of year, when leaves and bushes browned and shriveled before the grayness of winter set in. Everyone loved the fall, but she hated the cold. Spruce Mountain, Oregon, had all four seasons, and Natalie hated two. She crossed the street and stopped to pet a beautiful golden retriever waiting outside the craft store where she was headed on her lunch break.

"Look at you. You're so pretty. Are you Greta's new helper?" A tiny nagging feeling tugged at her when she noticed it wasn't wearing a collar. She gave the dog a quick rub with both hands as if to warm it and turned to march into the store to find out who had left their dog outside. She pushed the door open and smiled at the warmth that greeted her. "Greta, this is my favorite store on Main. It's always warm and smells like pumpkin bread."

Greta Bowman, owner of Creative Crafts, greeted her with a big smile. "Sheriff, you're always welcome here. Especially with the big drop in temperature today."

As sheriff of the small town, population 1,880, Natalie was hyperaware of anything out of the ordinary. She knew most of the residents and business owners. The town was comfortable, borderline boring, with the occasional public intoxication or disorderly conduct sprinkled in to keep her from doubting all her life choices and choosing a career that wasn't overly exciting. "I can't believe how cold it is. It's not even November. Do you know whose retriever that is out there?"

Greta looked around the store. "No, but we only have a few customers right now. Mrs. Bennett and another young woman. You can ask them." She pointed to the back of the store. "Let me go get your mother's order. I'll be right back."

Natalie nodded and worked her way over to Mrs. Bennett, who was perusing the yards of buffalo-check flannel.

"Oh, no, dear. That's not my dog. Brutus is home in bed. You remember Brutus, right?" Mrs. Bennett asked. She had a chihuahua she had carried in her purse until the dog's old bones couldn't handle the slight sway to-and-fro. Now Brutus stayed at home when she ran her errands.

"That sweet boy. Give him a pat on the head from me." The fact that Brutus was still alive surprised her. She remembered when he was an eight-week-old puppy. Back then, Mrs. Bennett was her physical-science teacher. She showed up at their high school graduation with him, much to the delight of everyone in attendance. Who could resist a puppy the size of a teacup? That was seventeen years ago. She smiled at Mrs. Bennett and circled the store to find the other patron Greta pointed out and located a petite brunette bent over a bin of buttons.

"Excuse me, miss? Is that your dog outside?" The brunette stood up and turned. Natalie took a step back and then another. She knew that face, those eyes, those full red lips. Time spun backward, and suddenly it was seventeen years ago, and she was at Ellie Shepherd's graduation party staring at the same soft brown eyes after experiencing the best kiss of her life.

"Oh, my God. Nat. Is that you?"

Warm hands grabbed hers and squeezed. Natalie blinked and stumbled over the words tumbling in her head. "Sarah. Hi. What are you doing here?" She clamped her mouth shut and forced a smile. "I mean, what brings you back to Spruce Mountain?"

Sarah Eastman was even more beautiful than the day she left. The innocence and softness of her youth had been replaced by stronger, more noticeable curves and a thinner, more mature face. Her beautiful dark hair now had caramel highlights and brushed her shoulders. Everything about her still took Natalie's breath away.

"I moved back to regroup. Spruce Mountain was always the closest thing to a home for me," Sarah said.

They were still holding hands. Natalie relaxed her grip and dropped the physical connection. "Your aunt and uncle still live here, right?" She knew the answer because she'd just seen them at the town meeting earlier in the month. Maintaining eye contact with Sarah was tough. She hated that all the confidence she'd built up over the last decade crumbled as she stood in front of the girl who'd kissed her once and never looked back.

"Yes. We're staying with them until we can find a place ourselves, or until I can figure out my life." Sarah tucked a piece of hair behind her ear with a shaky hand and broke eye contact.

The word "we" hit Natalie in the gut and caused her heart to slip down into her stomach. It wasn't as if she had pined for Sarah over the last twenty or so years of her life or compared every girlfriend she ever had to her, but Sarah had set the bar high the second their lips touched so many years ago. "Oh. That's great. I'm sure you'll figure something out." She told herself to quit nodding at Sarah. "I guess I'll see you around."

"Let's have lunch this week and get caught up."

"Sheriff? Are you in town? Fred just called. Said something happened at the market." Natalie's shoulder walkie-talkie boomed in the awkward silence that settled between them. Something always happened to Natalie when she got a call. The adrenaline rush kicked her confidence up a notch, and her heart, which was already beating at an alarming rate, fluttered faster. She reached up, pressed the button, and answered, fully aware she was still staring at Sarah. "I'm not too far away. I'll be there in ten." She released the button to end the call. "I'd better go. It's nice to see you again." Every part of her hummed with excitement, and a heated rush of anxiety flowed through her veins at seeing Sarah again.

Greta appeared. "Here's your mother's order. Be sure to tell her I said hello."

Greta's interruption gave Natalie an excuse to get out of there before she did or said anything stupid. She took the bag from Greta and nodded to both women as she created space. Spruce Market was within walking distance, but she couldn't go on a call with a giant bag of material slung over her shoulder. Plus, she needed time to process the last five minutes of her life.

Sarah Eastman was back in town. Sarah Fucking Eastman. The girl who had confused her and made love seem so clear at the same time when they were anything but. Why now? She hurried to where her car was parked, flooded with thoughts and memories of Sarah when life was easier and her emotions were untamed.

❖

"What's the problem, Fred?"

She stood taller when she was in uniform. The boots added a few inches, so when she met Fred at his office in the front of the store, she looked him straight in the eye. He wasn't a fan of female sheriffs and was vocal that he hadn't voted for her. But Natalie didn't feel threatened by him. His back had a slight hunch, and the skin on his arms swayed loosely past the short-sleeve button-up he wore. Fred was past his prime and had stopped caring about a lot since his wife died of cancer six years ago, two years after Natalie returned to Spruce Mountain. His nasty attitude was hard to swallow, but Natalie attributed it to loss of love and brushed it off whenever they interacted.

"There's a damn dog on the loose and was digging through the trash. Shredded some bags so there's garbage everywhere. Probably has rabies, too." A little bit of spittle bubbled up in the corner of his mouth.

Natalie looked away under the pretense of studying the few people sprinkled in the store. "Did you see the dog?"

Fred adjusted his pants and folded his arms. "Well, I didn't, but Tyler did."

"Where's Tyler? I'll need to talk to him."

"He's on break."

Natalie nodded. "Let's not bother him yet. Why don't you show me the trash cans?"

Fred motioned for her to follow him to the back of the store and unlocked the door that led to the two large dumpsters. One was supposed to be for recycling, but Fred never obliged and filled both with cardboard, rotting food, and things not from Spruce Market.

"Fred. Why don't you get your coat? It's cold outside."

He waved her off. "I'm fine." He pushed open the door and pointed to the only bag of garbage that was barely torn open at the bottom and left beside the dumpster. "See? Look at that. I'm going to start spraying my garbage with ammonia. That'll teach that mutt."

"Fred, I can't have you doing that. It's animal cruelty, and honestly, the mess here will take about thirty seconds to clean up."

He threw up his hands. "Are you going to do it, Sheriff?"

Natalie sighed. "I'm sorry you have to clean it up, but it's not bad. I'm sure Tyler will do it for you. I'll do my best to find the dog who did this to your trash."

Natalie bit her tongue at the flagrant abuse of the recycle bin. It was a constant battle with the trash company from Sawyer Disposal, the service from the next town. They took the recycled material away for free but charged customers for garbage. Fred was trying to circumvent the system by covering the top of the trash with layers of cardboard on pick-up days so he had to pay only the minimum. He'd been warned twice. The third violation would result in having the recycle bin removed and replaced with another trash dumpster. Sawyer Disposal gave her department a heads-up as a courtesy.

"So, you're telling me I can't protect my own property?"

"You call me, and we'll take care of it. No guns or harmful chemicals, Fred. Are we clear?"

He squinted his eyes with anger but slowly nodded. "Fine. But you need to find that dog."

"I will." Natalie checked her watch. "Is Tyler off his break yet?"

Fred opened the door for her and called out for Tyler, who jogged over to them.

"What's up?" He was slightly winded, and Natalie was disappointed as the smell of cigarette smoke wafted over her. He was seventeen and one of the few teenagers who wasn't on her radar as being a troublemaker.

"Tell me about the dog and what you saw exactly." Natalie pulled out her notepad. "Was it big, small, what color?"

Tyler bounced on the balls of his feet while he described the alleged rabid dog. "He was big and ran when I yelled at him. He got away with something, but I don't know what was in that bag." He shrugged.

"He?" Natalie asked.

Tyler nodded in confirmation.

"Did he seem threatening at all?"

Another shrug. "Not really. He just seemed skittish. Like he knew he was doing something wrong."

"Describe him, please."

"He was brown, with long hair and about this tall." Tyler held his hand down to mid-thigh, indicating the dog was good-sized.

"Wait. Did it look like a golden retriever?" At his blank stare, Natalie pulled up images of golden retrievers on her phone. She found a picture of a dog that looked just like the happy dog she'd met a few minutes ago. "Like this?"

Tyler pointed at the phone. "Yes. Just like that."

The dog that Natalie had met and petted twenty minutes ago was not a crazy, rabid dog. She turned to Fred. "Rabid?"

He motioned to Tyler. "Well, he was all excited when he told me. I was just delivering the message."

Tyler held up his hands and shrugged for the third time but wisely kept quiet.

Natalie flipped her notebook shut. "I will keep a lookout for the dog. If you see it, call me. In the meantime, get the trash cleaned up and put in the correct bin. Here's my card." She handed her business card to Tyler, dismissing Fred.

Natalie walked out of Spruce Market and looked down the street to the craft store. No cars were parked out front. Both Mrs. Bennett and Sarah were gone. The dog, the sweet golden retriever who'd wagged his tail back and forth when she rubbed his soft fur, had also disappeared. Was he there when she'd left the store in a hurry to get away from Sarah? She couldn't remember. Surely he belonged to someone. No animal that beautiful and sweet was a stray. The afternoon gave her a lot to think about. What was Sarah doing back in town, and who was missing a dog?

CHAPTER TWO

S arah sat down at her aunt's kitchen table with a cup of tea. "Natalie acted somewhat surprised, but she really didn't care to have lunch or anything." Sarah watched her spoon twirl and clank against the ceramic mug as she added honey.

"I don't believe that she didn't care. She was probably surprised. What did you tell her?"

Sarah had always admired her Aunt Judy. She was capable of making everyone feel like they were the most important person in the world. After she and Francine finally divorced, Aunt Judy and Uncle Bob didn't hesitate to invite her back to Spruce Mountain to regroup and create space after the less-than-amicable split. Sarah's parents were retired in the Philippines, where it was always warm and away from people. Even though their house was big, living with them wasn't a viable option. Vacationing with them was a definite, though.

"I told her we were back in town as kind of a new beginning, and she said good and then got a call and raced off." Even though Sarah had the upper hand because she was here and nobody really knew that yet, it was still a shock to come face-to-face with Natalie. It was bound to happen, but Sarah had hoped it would be more on her terms.

"Does she know who 'we' are? I mean, that word could

mean a wife, a husband, a girlfriend, a boyfriend, a pet, your parents, your college sorority. It covers a lot," Aunt Judy said.

"I barely remember our encounter other than she looked more beautiful today than she did in high school. But we both know I need to stay clear of everyone after what I just went through." Sarah reached for a cookie from the plate in the middle of the table. She groaned before taking a bite. "I've gained three pounds since I got here, and it's only been a week."

Her aunt shook her head. "Stop it. You look fine." She sat down and reached for the honey for her own cup of tea. "I've always liked Natalie. She was so quiet in school, but really blossomed when she returned to Spruce. She's been a great sheriff, and everyone seems to like what she's done for the town."

"I would like to catch up with her and anybody else still here."

Her aunt reached out and held Sarah's hands. "You've left the house only to enroll Harley in school. Why don't you let me watch her tonight, and you go out and unwind?"

"Aunt Judy, I don't even know where to go. I'm not great at meeting new people." Sarah blew across her tea before taking a sip.

"You have always been so happy and carefree. You have never had any problems making friends. A few people are still around who you might know. One of your old friends teaches at Harley's school. Brittany Wilson? Williams? You should look her up. And I don't know why you won't call Natalie."

Sarah had told her aunt about the kiss the night it happened, and her aunt had never forgotten. She was the only one in the family who knew Sarah was a lesbian as early as high school. She kept it quiet from the family, but her aunt was her one true confidante. It wasn't until Sarah met Francine and they moved in together that she finally came out to her parents. Her parents weren't thrilled, but they eventually tolerated Francine. They had mixed feelings when Harley was born. It wasn't that much of a surprise when they retired to the Philippines, since it had been their favorite vacation destination Sarah's entire life. They spoke on the phone and FaceTimed monthly, but it wasn't the same. Aunt Judy and Uncle Bob were accepting and supportive and loved Harley like she was their granddaughter.

"I don't think I'm ready to hang out with people."

Judy stood and held Sarah's face in her hands. "Okay. How about this? You and I will go out to Tanner's for a drink tonight. Bob can watch Harley. Girls' night out. What do you say?" When Sarah nodded her acceptance, Judy pinched her cheeks. "Atta girl. I'll let Bob know to be home by six."

"Don't interrupt his playtime. We'll go out when he gets home. Let him have his fun," Sarah said. Bob spent most of his afternoons at the Veteran's Lodge building things, playing cards, or organizing upcoming events in town. Judy spent her free time reading, hosting book clubs, and volunteering at the small hospital in Sawyer.

"He'll be fine. Any chance to spend time with Harley, and he'll be home early. You know he loves that little sweet angel so much."

"I'm so thankful for both of you. I don't know what I would do without you and Uncle Bob." Sarah's bank account was on the lean side after the divorce. She was going to have to find work somewhere soon. Probably not in Spruce Mountain, but in Portland, only a few hours away. A small town like Spruce Mountain didn't need another certified public accountant. She knew she could find a job in a heartbeat in a larger town, but right now she was still healing. Since Francine had never adopted Harley, they were able to leave Texas without any legal entanglements. Sarah had waited until the ink was dry on the divorce papers before she packed them up and headed to the Northwest.

"You know we would do anything for you and Harley. We're so happy you came back. You're welcome to stay as long as you like."

Sarah put her elbows on the table and rested her chin on her linked fingers. "I'm going stir-crazy. I need a job."

Judy dug through the recycle pile until she found the town newspaper that came out biweekly. "This is from three days ago. Let's look at the jobs available." She snapped open the paper to the Help Wanted section and read off the five ads. "Part-time bagger at Spruce Market. Evening shift."

"Nope."

"Okay. The next one is attendant at Lucky's Laundromat that pays minimum wage."

Sarah groaned and shook her head. "Nope."

"Oh, how about librarian? No experience necessary. And since it's next to the school, you can drop Harley off and then organize books or whatever."

Sarah sat up straighter. "That's not too bad. Circle that one."

"Honey, there are only five ads. I'm sure we'll be able to find it again."

"Point taken. What are the final two?"

Judy slipped her reading glasses back on and held the paper out. "Chuck's Chainsaw Cuts is looking for a bookkeeper, but I can't imagine why. I've seen the same artwork in his yard for months. Who knows? Maybe most of his work is online."

"Hard pass. My boss can't have access to anything that could possibly hurt me physically."

"It's too bad Hoffman's Mill shut down. That would have been a perfect place to work."

"I can't believe they just shut down like that." It was

because of that mill that Sarah's family had moved to Spruce Mountain. Uncle Bob got her dad a job there as a manager, and he ran a tight, profitable ship. When they closed a decade later, everyone was shocked.

"Honeybee Haven is looking for a beekeeper."

Sarah shook her head. "Again, my boss can't have access to anything that can kill me."

"You're not allergic to bees, are you?"

"No, but I don't want to get stung by a thousand either. I'll call the library and see if that job is available and what it pays."

"Don't feel like you need to get a place of your own right away. You and Harley have the entire downstairs. Like I said, you're welcome here for as long as you want."

It was as if Judy could read her mind. Sarah reached for the paper and flipped to the For Rent section. It was just as dismal and thin as the Help Wanted part. "Three apartments and two houses for rent. And sixteen houses for sale. The mill really wiped out a lot of tenants when it went out of business."

"It hit the community hard, but most of the businesses stayed." Judy shrugged and put her mug in the sink. "That's something, right?"

"True. But the schools are combined, right? Don't they bus the students over to Sawyer High School now?"

"Yes, but the middle-school students are bussed here. They moved into your old high school building. That gives them room and a soccer field they didn't have at Sawyer."

A wave of sadness and nostalgia washed over Sarah. High school really had been the best time of her life. Even though she was the new kid, people had accepted her, and she fell into the in crowd almost immediately. Now her school was gone, along with all her friends. It was as if her past had been erased.

"On second thought, I'll call the library in the morning or

swing by when I take Harley to school. Speaking of Harley, she's been very quiet." Sarah turned in the chair to see what her daughter was doing in the living room. She smiled and turned back around. "She's still working on that puzzle. She didn't get her patience from me, that's for sure."

"I'm going to text Bob. You go upstairs and get ready for our night out in this booming town," Judy said.

Sarah looked down at her oversized sweatpants and T-shirt that somebody gave her when they went to Florida, but she couldn't recall who. "What? I feel like I would fit in nicely."

"We're not going to Gravy's corner diner. Throw on some jeans and that nice red sweater. And maybe shower today."

Sarah gasped in jest. "What? Are you saying I stink?"

"No. I'm saying you'll feel better once you get cleaned up. And leave your hair down tonight. I love the length. It suits you well."

"I'm going to tame it before we leave. The world isn't ready for my hair in its natural state." The longer Sarah grew it, the wavier it got. She straightened it when she went out for a night out on the town, but that hadn't happened in so long. Where the hell was her flat iron? Packed away somewhere with all the other items she used to use to look good for somebody who never appreciated her efforts. She sighed after her internal mini pity party was over.

"But the world is ready for you, so let's go have a fun night."

"Is there an Uber or Lyft driver here in town?"

Aunt Judy laughed. "Yes. And you're looking at her."

"Come on. It's no fun if only I drink. And when was the last time you had more than a Shirley Temple or a second glass of wine?"

"We can always walk home. The bar is less than a mile away," Judy said.

"It's a cold day, and I doubt it'll warm up overnight. We'll both freeze out there, especially with the wind blowing as hard as it has all day." Sarah looked out the window at the gray sky that was darkening as night crept into town.

"We'll be fine. Go get ready. I'll start dinner for Harley and Bob."

Sarah kissed her aunt on the cheek and checked in with Harley before she bounced downstairs with excitement. She needed a night out, even if it was at a small local bar that probably had only six barstools, one pool table, and a television that played football games from the weekend before. She felt good about tonight, like it was a new beginning. Like something big was going to happen. Or maybe it was just the excitement of being an adult in a town she had left behind when she was still young.

Chapter Three

*H**i, Natalie. Would you like to join me and Sarah at Tanner's tonight around six?*

Natalie read the message on her phone and stood, causing the legs of her chair to screech across the linoleum floor. So much for discretion, she thought.

"Is everything okay, Boss?" David asked. He was second in command when Natalie was unavailable.

She sat and smiled to ease his obvious concern. "It's fine. I just got a text. That's all." She put her phone down and changed the subject so he wouldn't press. It was hard to have a private life in a small town. "Have we heard anything more about the stray dog?"

He shook his head. "Not really. Nobody has reported a missing dog in any of the nearby towns, and nobody here responded to our post. Not yet, at least."

Spruce Mountain's Sheriff's Department had an online system where the county could respond to questions designed specifically for this type of thing. Missing dog, missing cats, broken yard ornaments, and even a place where you could file a complaint anonymously. It was her deputy's job to keep an eye on it, and he informed her daily of anything new.

"Let's go ahead and do a blast to all the subscribers. I'll send you a generic picture of the dog and post that we are trying to find him." Natalie ignored the text message she'd just received and searched for the perfect golden-retriever photo. "Here. I found one. Say he's friendly but has been known to get into trash cans, so keep lids on tight and call or message us if they see him."

"On it, Boss."

When David called Natalie "boss," he meant it. He respected and borderline crushed on her. He was single, attractive, but a tad boring. He was a few years younger than her, and not once did he ever mention a hobby or anything other than movies. Classics, book-to-film movies, Oscar winners, B movies, and foreign films. He never talked about his family or anything normal, like renovations on the house he'd bought last year, or car problems, or great deals at Spruce Market. He talked only about movies. He was heavily involved in a movie-based online chat group that Natalie suspected he logged onto every night. Most single young men she knew gamed online, but David never mentioned Xbox or PlayStation. Her phone dinged again, and she looked at it in dread.

Please don't tell her I told you. I just think she needs a friend right now, and she's afraid to go out and find one.

Judy's first text inviting her to Tanner's had been a shock. The second one made sense. Her niece didn't know about the invite. Sarah had seemed only slightly surprised at seeing Natalie at Creative Crafts, as if it was a quick recognition and then disappointing realization it was only Natalie. She sighed. She should go see Sarah and say hi and get caught up and get it over with. It seemed as though she was in town for a bit, so running into her was going to happen, and Natalie wanted it to be on her terms for now. No more surprises.

She checked the time. Almost five. That gave her about an hour to get home, shower, and slip into clothes that were casual yet flattering. She wasn't sure if she wanted to be there early or show up fashionably late. Early. They could approach her instead of the other way around.

"I'm going to leave a few minutes early, but you can catch me on the radio." She grabbed her backpack and coat and headed out the back.

"Oh, hot date tonight?" Faith had been with the department only eighteen months. They had needed a receptionist, and Faith had needed a job after her third marriage tanked.

Natalie hesitated as she reached for the doorknob. "Uh, no. Just things to do." She flashed Faith a smile and closed the door behind her, but not before she heard Faith yell out. "Don't forget to run the material to your mom."

Shit, Natalie thought. That was going to set her back at least ten minutes. She called her mom when she got in the car.

"Mom, hi. Listen. I'm running late and am meeting friends at Tanner's tonight. Can I run the material over tomorrow morning, and we can have coffee?" Natalie was immediately wracked with guilt. Her mom didn't get out much since her dad lost his battle with cancer eight years ago. "Scratch that. Better idea. How about you join me for drinks tonight at Tanner's?"

"Oh, no, sweetheart. I'm not ready to go out."

Natalie could visualize her mother tugging on the back of her hair, already worried about how she looked. "I'll go home and get changed. Be ready in forty-five minutes. I won't take no for an answer." She hung up so her mother couldn't back out.

The drive home took only five minutes. She pulled out a black sweater and dark jeans while stripping off her uniform and took a ten-minute shower. She shaved in places she hadn't in a long time, but not because she thought anything would happen. It just made her feel sexy and confident when she was smooth. She wasn't able to dry her hair all the way because lack of time was frantically pushing her through the door.

Early was still better than late. She tugged on her ankle boots while dabbing makeup on her face. After a quick inspection and a few swipes of a mascara brush, she grabbed her lip gloss and her coat, and raced out to her Jeep.

It was a quarter to six. She was never going to make it. It would take five minutes to get to her mom's house, five minutes to get her mother ready, and five minutes to get to Tanner's. Best-case scenario, they would arrive at the same time as Judy and Sarah. She backed out of her driveway and smacked her hand on the steering wheel. "Shit." She put the Jeep in park, raced over to her sheriff's vehicle, and grabbed her mom's bag of material. The whole thing took about twenty seconds off the clock, but it felt like minutes.

Much to her surprise, Natalie's mother, Linda, was waiting for her at the door. "Honey, do you have to drive that fast? I mean, I know you're the sheriff and all, but you aren't being careful tearing into the driveway like that."

She ran to the passenger side and helped her mother into the car. "I know. I know. I'm just trying to beat the crowd. Listen, Mom. Judy Eastman secretly invited us because her niece, Sarah, is back in town, and she wants her to feel welcome. She remembered that we knew one another and asked that we meet them up there without knowing that she planned it. Can you do that?"

Linda stared at her daughter. "The same Sarah who kissed you and pretended she didn't and then left and never answered your texts? That one?"

"Mom, we were young and confused. Truthfully, she probably did forget. We consumed a lot of alcohol that night."

Linda put her hands over her ears. "I'm not supposed to know these things."

Natalie reached over and tapped her mom's leg until she moved her hands. "Mom, it was a long time ago. I've already forgotten." She hadn't, though. Sarah showed up in her thoughts when she least expected her to, like when she read a book that tugged at her heartstrings, or saw a gray kitten like the fluffy gray kittens Sarah loved, or when she saw lilies in somebody's garden. Lilies were Sarah's favorite. She doodled them everywhere: on her notebook, in the margins of her textbooks, and even on the condensation that gathered on her car windshield when the seasons changed to cooler temperatures.

And there was always the first kiss with anybody new. Not that Natalie had a lot of those, but she always compared each first kiss to her first kiss with Sarah. Natalie couldn't help it. Most first kisses were awkward, but that one special night, with that one special girl, her first kiss was perfect. Just thinking about it kicked her heartbeat up a few notches.

"It's a good thing Judy will be there. She'll make it not so uncomfortable for you both."

Natalie rolled her eyes. "Mom, I'm fine."

Linda pointed to Natalie's death grip on the steering wheel. "I haven't seen you this tense in a really long time. You aren't still carrying a torch for her, are you?"

Loosening her grip on the steering wheel, Natalie sat back in the seat and managed to bark out a small laugh. "Carry a torch? Mom, we need to modernize your lingo."

"Deflection. I invented it."

Natalie turned the corner and found an empty spot on the street. "Oh, look. We're here." She batted her eyelashes at her mom and jumped out of the car.

"We'll talk about this later."

Natalie waited for her mother and linked arms with her. "Nah. Let's just have a nice mother-daughter night."

"You mean mother-daughter-and-the-girl-who-got-away night?"

"And yes, her too, if we're going to be technical." Natalie held the door for her mother and took a deep breath before she looked around the town's only bar. Tanner's looked exactly the same as it had the night she returned to Spruce Mountain eight years ago and had a much-needed drink with her father. It was the night he told her the history of himself, all the things she didn't know. It was a night of extremes. Extreme happiness at the memories they had, and extreme sadness when they knew he wouldn't be around for Christmas. Nothing could keep the cancer from spreading, so he stopped treatments and spent the last few weeks saying his good-byes to the people he loved most.

Natalie shook her head at the memory and turned her attention to the patrons who dotted the place. Four booths with high-back green cushions lined one side of the bar from the front door to the kitchen area. A dozen mismatched barstools were pressed under the L-shaped bar, and a pool table that was entirely too big for the establishment filled up most of the free space. They served peanuts, pretzels, and sometimes popcorn in little wooden bowls at the bar, but people weren't here to eat. They were here to drink. Tanner's had a great selection of whiskey and surprisingly good beer on tap. It wasn't a place Natalie frequented, but on rough days, she swung by for a quick beer and a handful of pretzels. Sometimes that was her dinner. She always left a bigger tip on those sad evenings.

"Well, speak of the devil," Linda said, her voice low enough for only Natalie to hear.

"Hi. What are you ladies doing here? Come join us." Judy waved them over to the booth. She scooted over, and Linda immediately sat down next to her. There was only one place left to sit. Natalie watched as Sarah slid over to make room for her. She clenched her teeth and smiled at Sarah when she sat down.

"We thought we'd come out for a quick drink. Natalie's been working so hard and needed to get out for a bit," Linda said.

"Hi, Nat. It's good to see you again. We were kind of rushed earlier."

Natalie couldn't stop the flush from spreading up her neck and over her cheeks. The emotional tailspin she was in gave her a moment of nausea, and she could only smile weakly at Sarah.

"Sarah, what brings you back to Spruce? Last I remember, you were down in Texas, right?" Linda quickly ordered a domestic beer on tap from the waitress, who came out of nowhere. Natalie ordered a Heineken, and Sarah and Judy asked for glasses of wine.

"Yes. I went to school down there and ended up staying."

Natalie was already dreading Sarah's story. She had probably met some guy, married him after college, and started the perfect family. Her eye roll must have been visible because she felt a warning kick under the table from her mom. Judy either didn't see it or pretended not to notice. "You studied finance, right?" She always remembered Sarah beating her in algebra and economics.

"I'm a CPA. Not really a need for one of those in town, since Spruce already has one," she said.

"If you're looking to stay, I'm sure you could set up shop here. Brian Denmore can't do it all. A little competition is good," Linda said.

Sarah cocked her head as if the idea had merit. "You know, if I can't find anything, I might consider that. Tomorrow I'm going to the library. Apparently, they need help, and it's right next door to the elementary school, so I could drop Harley off and then go to work."

"Do you have only one child?" Linda asked.

Natalie stared straight ahead, completely hating this line of questioning. She was so close to Sarah that they bumped elbows and smiled apologetically at one another.

"Yes, a six-year-old daughter. Harley. The love of my life."

"She's been a blessing for me and Bob. We just love her to death," Judy said. She pulled out her phone to show the table photos of Harley.

"She looks just like you," Natalie said. For the first time since sitting next to her, she looked Sarah in the eye.

Sarah looked down. "She's my mini me. Only her hair is lighter and straighter than mine."

Natalie remembered tugging on a piece of hair playfully right before they kissed. She sighed. That was a long time ago. And Sarah didn't even remember. It was time to forget about the past and just move forward. "Is she in kindergarten?"

"No. She's in first grade."

It was hard for Natalie to focus on anything but Sarah's lips. She watched them as Sarah described taking Harley to her first day of school and how well she seemed to be adjusting.

"I think one of the elementary teachers is somebody who graduated one year ahead of us. Rebecca Palmer. Do you remember her?" Natalie asked.

"Oh, great." Sarah sat back in the booth and sighed.

"What? That bad?"

Sarah nodded and laughed. "I stole her boyfriend."

"Oh, my God. That's right. You blew into town and took Brent away from her the first week you were here." Natalie grabbed a handful of pretzels to keep her hands busy. Being this close was making her antsy.

"Well, I don't know that I did that, but what was I thinking?

He was awful. He partied too hard and treated everyone like crap."

Natalie sat up a little taller when Sarah's fingers brushed hers as they both reached for pretzels. "Sorry," she mumbled and quickly moved her fingers away.

"What ever happened to Brent?"

"Let's just say he peaked in high school," Natalie said. Brent had worked at the mill with his father, and when it closed, Brent had found odd jobs around town until he exhausted all possibilities. The last Natalie had heard, he was in Portland working at a vintage record store.

"What a waste of time that was, huh?" Judy asked, and winked at Sarah.

"Because we don't know if he was successful?" Linda jumped into the conversation, having finished scrolling through Judy's photos of Harley.

"She means because I'm a lesbian, and I was trying to be somebody I wasn't in high school."

Sweat popped up on the back of Natalie's neck and on her palms. The longneck she was holding slipped out of her hand and smacked on the tabletop, spilling the contents in the direction of Judy's lap. She jumped up and slapped napkins in the path of the liquid. "Shit. I'm sorry." She glanced at her mom, who quirked her eyebrow.

"It's okay." Judy waved off the handful of spare napkins. Natalie and her long reach stopped the beer from spilling onto Judy's lap. "At least you aren't drinking red wine."

Natalie couldn't decide if her phone ringing at this exact moment was a blessing or a curse. "Sheriff Strand."

"Sheriff, we have a sighting on the dog." David's voice was filled with excitement.

"Did someone call?" Natalie turned around so her back

was to Sarah, and she plugged her other ear with her finger to hear him better. "Or did someone post?"

"Jim Pierce called and said he saw a dog fitting that description in his shop garage."

"That's not too far from here. Let me head out and see if I can find it." Natalie clicked off her phone and stood. "I'll be right back. There's a loose dog we've been trying to catch."

"So, you're the sheriff, dogcatcher, welcoming committee. So many hats, Natalie," Sarah said.

Natalie shrugged. "When I come back, I'll share some interesting stories of being a sheriff in a small town. I shouldn't be long." She slipped on her coat and bolted out the door.

Jim was exactly like Fred at Spruce Market and would probably shoot the dog if it didn't vacate his property. She pulled up at the exact time she heard a gunshot. Her fear flipped to anger immediately. She threw open the car door, turned on her high beams so Jim didn't accidentally shoot her, and barked out for him. "Jim. Sheriff Strand. Put down that shotgun." Nobody answered, so she put on her flashing lights and used the loudspeaker. "Damn it, Jim. Can you hear me?"

"Yeah, yeah. I hear you. My gun's down."

Natalie cautiously approached him. "Jim. You can't fire a gun in town. I should write you up." Even though he lived on the outskirts, it was still illegal, and it pissed her off. That dog was probably scared to death.

"I have every right to protect my property."

"It's a fucking domesticated dog who's lost. If I hear you shoot a gun or if you kill it, I'm hauling your ass to jail for animal abuse." Natalie was furious, and keeping her anger tamped down and remaining professional was incredibly difficult. She had never liked Jim, because he was always trying to cause trouble but knew exactly how to stay a hair on the right side of the law. Except for firing a shotgun.

"I called the department five minutes ago."

"I came as soon as I got the message. When we posted to keep an eye out for the dog, it didn't mean to shoot it." She took his shotgun and put it in her car. "It stays here until I'm done searching the property." Natalie grabbed a tactical flashlight, locked her car, and shined the sharp beam of light down the driveway that led to Jim's garage and shop.

Jim followed, keeping a good ten feet between them. "I just saw him when you pulled in. He was in my shop, and then when I fired the gun in the air, he ran to the back of the shop."

He stumbled over the in-the-air part of his explanation. Natalie ignored him and walked around the whole shop but didn't see the dog. She booted open the side door where the dog had entered and escaped, according to Jim. It was probably looking for shelter. She hunched her shoulders against the cold she suddenly felt now that her anger at Jim was subsiding. "I'm going to look in the woods. I want you to stay here in case he returns." At his nod, she turned back around and shined her flashlight in the tall trees. She saw paw prints, but they were spread all out as if the dog purposely did it to throw her off, or nervously pranced because he was scared of the shotgun but didn't know where to go.

Her heart broke. "Oh, baby boy. Where are you?" She walked through the woods for a good twenty minutes before returning to Jim's gravel driveway. "I didn't see him, but I did see some dog prints. Listen, the dog isn't going to hurt you or destroy your property. I'll give you back your gun and not write you a citation if you promise not to shoot it. Call us if he shows up again." She seriously doubted he would.

"It's a ghost dog. I have no idea where it could go other than deeper into the woods, and if that's the case, you can forget about it. It'll never find its way out," Jim said.

"I mean it. Don't shoot the dog." She handed him back

his gun and climbed into her car. She kept eye contact with him until she reached the end of the driveway. As much as she wanted to get back to Tanner's, she had to at least drive around the neighborhood to see if the dog was anywhere else. It was the first sighting of him since this afternoon. After driving up and down several long driveways, she gave up. There was no sign of Ghost Dog, and she needed to get back to her mother and, if she was being truthful, back to hear Sarah's story. Dropping a bomb like that deserved all her attention. Worst-case scenario, she would get the details from her mother.

"You're back. We're all on second rounds. Do you want another Heineken?" Judy asked when Natalie slipped back in the booth.

"No, thank you, but I could use a hot tea. It's cold out there."

Linda reached out and held Natalie's hands to warm them. It was a sweet gesture. "You were gone for a bit. Did you find the dog?"

Natalie shook her head and frowned. She told them the story of the dog, but left out the part about Jim shooting at it. Neither he nor she needed the grief these women would rain down on Jim for shooting at somebody's pet. Hoping they would pick up where they left off, Natalie asked, "What did I miss?"

CHAPTER FOUR

Sarah closed the door softly behind her and locked it. It was almost midnight, and they were trying to be quiet so as to not wake Uncle Bob or Harley.

"Come here and look at this." Aunt Judy motioned for Sarah.

"He's going to spoil her, isn't he?" Sarah took a photo of Harley asleep on Uncle Bob's lap, completely unaware of his loud snoring. She watched the rise and fall of Harley's little body in the crook of Uncle Bob's arm and sighed. It was adorable, even though it sounded like Uncle Bob was revving a car before the start of a drag race.

"How can she sleep so hard?" Aunt Judy asked.

"She doesn't know anything bad in this world. She's innocent. I wish I could sleep this well." Sarah scooped Harley up, careful not to wake her. Bob stirred when the weight was lifted off him.

Judy whispered in his ear so he wouldn't be startled. "Go to bed, Bob." Bob blinked a few times until he focused. He was slow to rise out of the chair but eventually worked his way up the stairs to the bedroom. Judy turned to Sarah. "Go put Harley to bed and come up. Let's talk about the night."

Sarah needed to talk to someone to release the buildup of excitement that sat in her chest at being back in town and seeing Natalie again after so many years. She tucked Harley into her bed, turned on the small lamp across the room, and tiptoed out. Judy handed her a cup of hot cocoa with a top layer of melted mini marshmallows. Sarah wrapped her hands around it, enjoying the warmth on her fingers.

"It sure was nice to hang out with Natalie and Linda," Judy said.

"Nat was a bit standoffish."

Judy gave her a look. It wasn't quite a smirk, but more of a "tell me something I didn't know" look. "Well, can you blame her?"

"Come on. It was a long time ago. Plus, I don't think she remembers." Sarah looked down at her cocoa, knowing full well Judy was studying her.

"Of course she remembers. She was stiff straight the entire first drink. A bit more relaxed when she returned from her call about the stray dog. She looks great, and she's doing such a good job with the town."

"She looks fantastic. Even prettier than she did in high school."

"She grew into herself. She found confidence somewhere along the way. And did you hear what Linda said? She's not dating anyone."

Sarah squelched the desire to fantasize about Natalie. The tiny flame that had reignited and sparked in the pit of her stomach upon seeing Natalie again was hard to ignore, but she had just finalized her divorce, and dating wasn't a great idea. Focusing on Harley and getting normalcy back in her life was her number-one priority. She could put her own desires on hold. "You know that's not a good idea. Plus, I don't want to be that parent who dates a ton of people while my daughter watches and learns from my behavior."

Judy threw up her hands. "You're not asking Natalie to

move in. You're just planning to do things with her that don't include Harley. That's how single parents date. They hire a babysitter, who would be me and I'm cheap, and go out on dates and have fun and make out. Don't close yourself off because you think you don't deserve happiness, because you do."

Sarah had been in only three serious relationships as an adult. She'd dated a guy in college who treated her like a queen, but she didn't feel anything when they kissed or made love. She broke it off to be fair to both of them. When she'd finally accepted that she was a lesbian, she had one long-term relationship after a series of horrific first and second dates. Then her life had changed when she met Francine nine years ago.

"Even though we've been separated for a year and recently divorced, I still feel like I'm a part of that family. It sounds crazy, but I feel guilty if I find somebody else attractive. I need to switch my mind from married to single." She scooped a spoonful of marshmallows into her mouth and grimaced. "Ugh. These are too sweet. How Harley can eat them is beyond me." She poked a hole in the soft, sugary shell that encased the hot chocolate to get to the liquid, which promptly burned her tongue. "Ow. Really?"

"Who struggles with hot chocolate?" Judy traded cups with Sarah. "Here. Take mine. Now, let's get back to our conversation. You should ask Natalie out. Or even just to hang out and get a better feel for her. We didn't find out a lot, other than she's not dating anyone. After Natalie left on that call, Linda made sure we knew that."

"I guess I could always use a friend. And Nat was always nice to me. Maybe I'll swing by the department in a day or so and drop off cookies or something small-town like that," Sarah said.

"Everybody there will appreciate it, and you both could use a new friend."

When she was younger, Sarah had easily made friends. They weren't the ever-lasting kind though. They were the cliques, the partygoers, the people she had lunch with and, over time, simply stopped calling or texting. They weren't the people she turned to in her time of need. Sarah longed for a friendship that had depth. Moving around her whole life had made one like that almost impossible to have. "I have an idea. Thank you for the suggestion." Sarah drained her mug and kissed her aunt on the cheek. "I'm going to bed. Tonight was fun but also exhausting."

"Sleep well, dear."

Sleep didn't come easy to Sarah. Natalie was the only thing on her mind. She was even more beautiful than Sarah remembered. Tall, gorgeous, and confident. She was such a fool in high school. The night at Ellie's party had confused her. Vodka and cherry 7UP was her poison.

She had been on her third when she saw Natalie sitting on the fireplace, drink in hand but not sipping on it, trying to be as inconspicuous as an awkward seventeen-year-old shy blonde could be in a sea of popular kids. It was so obvious she didn't want to be there, didn't belong there, didn't want to be noticed, but Sarah noticed. She smiled and headed over to Nat, thinking she was being suave, but as she recalled, she moved with the grace of an elephant. She leaned into Nat's personal space and touched her hair, telling her it was the most beautiful color she'd ever seen. In the span of thirty seconds, she not only invaded Nat's private time, but she touched her without consent.

She groaned when she recalled leaning across her lap to pretend interest in what Nat was drinking. It was a flirty ploy to get even closer. Without thinking, she brushed her lips over

Nat's in a whisper of a kiss. When Nat didn't move, Sarah kissed her for the first time in a dark corner of Ellie Shepherd's living room. She pulled Natalie's bottom lip into her mouth and ran her tongue over it and moaned when she felt Natalie's hands in her hair. Natalie kissed her back smoothly, as though she'd been expecting Sarah to do it. She was in shock at how intense it was and at the jolt of pleasure that rippled through her body. Years later, it was still her best kiss ever. She put her fingers to her lips, thinking about missed opportunities and how Natalie was the one who got away.

❖

"Oh, my God. Sarah Eastman. Is that really you?"

Sarah closed the door behind her and smiled. She remembered Faith from the cheerleading squad a few years behind her in school. She looked the same except for several laugh lines around her eyes and small, vertical lines above her top lip from a bad habit, which showed when she didn't smile. How Faith could be sitting near the front door in a sleeveless blouse was crazy. Sarah subconsciously pulled up her turtleneck for more warmth.

"It's me. I'm back." Sarah shrugged and glanced around the room. She stopped herself from frowning when she realized Natalie wasn't there. "I came to drop off some cookies to the department and say hi to Natalie."

Just then, Natalie blew into the common area, obviously unaware she had company. "We got another call on Ghost Dog. I'm headed out to see if I can round him up."

Sarah watched as she tucked her hair behind her ears and set her campaign hat firmly on top of her head. Time had been good to Natalie. The department's drab khaki uniform couldn't hide her curvy body, much to Sarah's delight. A small tremble worked its way from somewhere deep inside her, traveled up through her throat, and escaped her mouth in the form of a small sigh at how beautiful Natalie was. It wasn't loud enough for Natalie to hear, but Faith obviously heard and loudly cleared her throat.

"Hey, Boss. You have a visitor."

Sarah froze when Natalie's gaze met hers. A flash of something in Natalie's eyes momentarily confused her. It was a combination of anger and passion. Then Natalie softened and smiled.

"Sarah, hi. What are you doing here?"

Tongue-tied at their moment that had happened in a flash, Sarah could only smile and thrust the plate of cookies at her.

"Did you bake these?"

After two seconds of awkward silence, she found her voice. "Harley and I did last night. I just dropped her off at school and thought I'd pop in and see if you were around." Why was she so nervous? Seeing Natalie in action doing her job gave her chills. The quiet woman who had sat next to her a few nights ago had become someone who wielded power and determination.

"That's so sweet. Thank you. I'm going out to look for that dog, if you want to come with me. I need to head out while the lead's still hot."

As much as she wanted to, getting a job was more important. "I can't. I'm going to apply at the library this morning. I tried yesterday, but the person who does the hiring was out sick." Sarah excused herself, feeling Natalie's restrained energy at small talk. "I'll talk to you later. Go find that dog."

"I'll walk you out."

Sarah felt a jolt of energy when Natalie barely touched the small of her back as she led her through the front door.

"Thanks again. That'll be my lunch." Natalie thumbed behind her at the office.

"Well, if you want something more substantial and definitely healthier, give me a call. We can have lunch without our family."

"Here. Put your number in my phone." Natalie handed it to Sarah and waited while she fumbled around until she got all the digits right and her name spelled correctly. She was a hot mess and hoped Natalie didn't pick up on it.

"Okay. Now go do sheriff stuff." Sarah gave Natalie her prettiest smile and climbed into her car. She took a deep breath and slowly made her way to the library. Even though she kept telling herself a relationship wasn't a good idea and she wanted to focus on Harley and getting her situated and comfortable in a new place, Natalie was making her feel things she hadn't in a long time.

Now that she had given Natalie her phone number, she was going to check it a lot more for messages. She didn't talk to anybody daily, so texting wasn't on her radar. And social media? Since her divorce, she'd stopped posting online. Most of her accounts were of a happy family who didn't exist anymore. It wasn't that important. She had a strong core with her aunt, uncle, and Harley, and it was crucial that Harley not be affected by the transition to single parent. She was so focused on getting her daughter settled that it never sank in that she, too, was getting a fresh start.

❖

"The job is Monday through Friday, nine until two. And Saturdays if you want, but usually we can get someone to pick up that shift. The job doesn't pay much, but you can read all you want during your shifts, as long as the work gets done. We now have a great selection of audiobooks. Do you enjoy reading?" Mary Cooper, head librarian, said.

"I love reading." Sarah guessed Mary to be in her mid-sixties. She was fascinated with Mary's long, graying hair that she parted down the middle and rolled into buns right above both ears. It wasn't really a Princess Leia thing from *Star Wars*, but damn close. She was mesmerized by how straight Mary's part was, and her eyes kept straying to the stark-white line when the conversation lulled, which happened a lot.

Two dollars above minimum wage wasn't great, but it was something. If she needed more money, she could take Judy's advice and open a small practice. Tax season was coming up, and maybe she could work on returns in the afternoons after her shift at the library. This was a blessing and gave her time with Harley before and after school. "I would love the job. It works great with my schedule." She'd already told Mary that she had a daughter at the elementary school and assured her that she had help at home if Harley missed school because of a cold or a doctor's appointment.

"When can you start?"

Sarah didn't hesitate. "I can sign on the dotted line today."

CHAPTER FIVE

How is this dog everywhere and nowhere at the same time?" Natalie rubbed her hands together and blew on them to keep them warm. She rested her hip against the bull bar of her cruiser and looked at Joshua Monroe, one of her deputies, who only shrugged. They both had arrived at Mrs. Wanda Jenkins's house at the same time, but neither saw the golden retriever. Mrs. Jenkins swore it had run out into the road two seconds before they arrived.

"It was right there. I saw it digging in my mums. I called you right away, just like your post asked."

Mrs. Jenkins was an eighty-one-year-old widow who wore tinted thick glasses and had a pronounced limp, a result of rheumatoid arthritis that had settled in her knee. Most of the time she stayed indoors, but every so often, the postal carrier would forget to bring her mail to the door, and she would have to shuffle down the steps to the mailbox or collect the newspaper that nobody could remember to deliver by hand. She called the sheriff's department to complain about this or that, but the conversation always turned to something else. Spruce Market's delivery service was subpar and somebody should tell Fred, or that the new stylist, Amanda Pritz, who made house calls, was fabulous. Judging by her fluffed-up hair, Wanda had recently had it done.

Natalie walked over to the freshly disturbed dirt where Mrs. Jenkins said the dog had rooted around, kicked the dirt back into place, and tamped it with her boot. "Well, do you want to divide and conquer? I'll head north and you head south. Let's start on foot. That way we can weave in and out of the houses better. That dog couldn't have gotten far if Mrs. Jenkins said it crossed the road right before we showed up." She was already tired, and it wasn't even lunchtime.

"Golden retriever, right?" Joshua asked.

Natalie liked Joshua. He was young, eager, and didn't mind working eleven to seven every day. She, Joshua, David, and Betty, the overnight deputy, rotated working weekends. Crime never slept, so somebody was always on duty.

"Yes. And contrary to popular belief, he's really friendly."

"I've never known one who wasn't. Check in." Joshua pointed to his shoulder walkie-talkie and headed in the opposite direction, whistling and yelling "Here, boy" every ten seconds. He took his job seriously and Natalie admired that. He would make a good sheriff one day, after he had a little more experience. She didn't whistle like Joshua did, but called out from time to time as she walked down every driveway and looked under stoops and over fences.

"I see him. He's behind the house on Fir and Juniper. One-oh-eight Juniper." Joshua's message on the walkie made her quickly turn around. She ran to his location.

"Joshua. Joshua." She looked around for signs of him or the dog but saw neither. She clicked on her walkie. "Where are you?" She walked around to the back of the house where Joshua was half under the crawl space of the house.

"He's here. I found him." Joshua wiggled out from the tight space and pointed. "He's somewhere under the house." He stood and brushed dirt and leaves from his once-pressed uniform. "How are we going to get him out?"

Natalie squatted and looked through the lattice that was partially pushed back. She pulled out her flashlight and looked all around. "Are you sure? I don't see—" She heard a screeching sound. "Okay. Holy shit. That's probably the biggest marmot I've ever seen in my life." She stood and took a few steps back. "Maybe you were wrong? That's not a golden retriever."

Joshua bent and looked. "No. I swear he was there. I didn't see the marmot at all. Jesus, he's a big one, isn't he?" He gave a low whistle.

Natalie let out a sigh. She didn't want to have to call in animal control. They had a habit of taking everything not tied down. Spruce Mountain had several pets that got out for simple reasons, like they slipped through the fence or a child left the front door open and didn't realize Fifi got loose. It was a small, tight-knit community, and the neighbors worked together to ensure they were safe, pets were taken care of, and people had what they needed. It was one reason Natalie stayed, regardless of the Freds and Jims in the world.

"Okay. I'll radio dispatch. Why don't you knock on the door and see if anyone is home and tell them what's happening?" If the dog was under there, it was trapped and possibly not safe with the marmot under there, too. She circled the house and found a small section that wasn't blocked off and examined the opening. She pulled away a few short yellow and brown hairs but wasn't sure if it was the retriever's hair or if this was even his entrance or exit or both. For all she knew, she was holding a tuft of marmot fur. She dropped it and wiped her hands on her pants.

"Listen, doggo, if you are under there, you need to come out before animal control gets here. You can hang out in the warm car, and you might even have a cheeseburger in your future if you come out." Natalie listened but didn't hear anything. She joined Joshua, who informed her nobody was home, or at least not answering the door.

"The crawl space must be the entire length of the house. Except for the deck," Joshua said.

"Maybe that's how Ghost Dog is getting in and out. I wonder if this is his hiding place."

"Do you think the marmot would share the space? He seems awful big and mean," Joshua said.

"I'd like to believe that animals take care of one another, just like people do. Even R.O.U.S.," Natalie said. She smiled at Joshua's confused look. "What? You don't know what R.O.U.S. is?" She laughed. "David would."

Joshua turned his head and clicked the walkie-talkie to life. "Calling Sly. Come in, Sly Stallone. I have a question the boss said you can answer." David got the nickname because the department found out he saw *Rambo* thirty-four times, not because he was a boxer or gym rat.

"Oh, this is going to be good." David laughed. "Hit me."

"What does R.O.U.S. stand for?"

"Are you dealing with an R.O.U.S. right now?" David asked. He whistled just like Joshua had a few minutes ago.

"Would somebody please tell me what it means?" Joshua said.

"Rodents of Unusual Size. It's from the movie *The Princess Bride*, circa 1987."

"Holy crap. You should see what we're dealing with here. I've never seen a marmot this big before. It's got to be a solid ten pounds."

"I thought you were after the dog?" David's voice cracked across the walkie.

"We got sidetracked. The dog might still be under the house with the R.O.U.S. We're waiting on animal control," Natalie said.

"Ouch. Keep an eye out on them. They aren't known for their gentleness with animals."

Natalie piped in. "I'm here to make sure nothing bad happens." If Natalie wasn't good at her job or didn't like being the sheriff of Spruce Mountain and the surrounding county, she would have returned to Colorado and worked at a place for animals like the local shelter or The Pet Posh Inn, which had just opened locations in Denver and Colorado Springs. Animals were important to her, and even though she thought she was too busy to have one, she did what she could to help them.

While they waited, Natalie wasn't entirely convinced the dog was still under the house, so she walked around the property and along the outskirts of the woods behind the neighborhood to look for him.

"Sheriff, animal control is here." Joshua's voice startled her a bit in the quiet of the forest.

She pinched the button on the speaker. "On my way. Two minutes." She hustled back to the house to greet the officer. "Hi, I'm Sheriff Strand. We're looking for a dog, a pet of a friend's, and we think he might be under the house. In the process, we found an R.O.U.S. living on the south end."

"An R.O.U.S.? Let me adjust the noose." She increased the size of the opening.

"Does everybody know what an R.O.U.S. is except for me?" Joshua threw up his hands.

Without smiling, the officer responded. "In this line of business, you learn it on day one. Besides, it was my favorite movie growing up. What's your friend's dog's name?"

Natalie froze. She didn't want the dog to be caught in that frightening way, nor did she want him to be taken away. He was so beautiful and obviously somebody's pet. She hadn't been expecting to have to come up with a name to go with her lie and blurted out the first thing that came to her mind. "Milford."

"Milford?" Joshua asked.

Natalie avoided eye contact with Joshua and waved her hand. "Apparently it's a family name. He answers to Ford." Worst dog name ever, she thought. "Don't ask me the marmot's name because we aren't on friendly terms." That warranted a laugh from everyone and got the attention back on the marmot.

"I need you all to step back."

The officer slipped on paper coveralls and a headlamp with three flashlights, which almost blinded Natalie when she flipped them on. Natalie stepped back, pulling Joshua with her. "I know you are curious, but I don't need you to get bitten by the marmot." They waited for about five minutes until a scuffle ensued and the officer backed out slowly.

"Got him. Yep. He's big all right." She pulled the long pole with the largest marmot Natalie had ever seen tethered to the end. They backed away farther when she swung the marmot around to deposit him in the big carrier in back. Natalie snapped a quick picture because nobody was going to believe them. She sent the photo to Sarah.

Look at this chubby marmot!

Fat-shaming a marmot. Tsk, tsk, Nat. Who does that? Sarah followed it with a winking emoji. *And holy crap, he really is giant.*

Welcome to Spruce Mountain, where the marmots are big as dogs.

Natalie focused back on the animal-control officer. "Did you see the dog under the house by chance?" Natalie asked after the marmot was behind bars.

"No, but I'm going to take another look around. Make sure there aren't any babies." She flipped on the headlamp again and disappeared under the house.

With the marmot safely caged, Natalie walked around the house to the opening she'd found earlier. No action there. It was completely quiet, except for the officer who was scooting under the house. Where did the dog go?

"Nothing else is under there. No nests, no dogs, no cats. Nothing." After ripping off her paper coveralls, the officer climbed into the truck.

"What's going to happen with him?" Natalie leaned closer to the open window and thumbed behind her.

"We'll find a place far away where he can make a better home and not endanger any people."

"Great. Thanks for coming out." She tapped her hand on the car door dismissively and walked to Joshua. "Well, at least we accomplished something today."

"Milford? What's the story there?"

Natalie shrugged. "I feel like he's somebody's dog, and I don't want him going to animal control and getting pulled farther away from his home. He might not be from here, but somebody has to be missing him."

"I get that, but couldn't you come up with a better name than Milford? Like Rigsby or Baxter?" Joshua asked.

"Does it really matter? Come on. Let's get back to the office."

❖

Natalie spent the afternoon filling out forms and purchase orders, and eating six of the cookies Sarah dropped off. They were just the way she liked cookies—crispy crusts with soft centers. She picked up her phone and sent Sarah a text without even thinking.

These are store bought, aren't they? Because nobody bakes this well.

Natalie smiled at the bubbles.

It was hard to get Harley to wash her hands every single time she wanted to taste the dough.

Three hundred and seventy-five degrees will kill all germs. We're good.

Was that your lunch?

I plead the fifth. Natalie looked at the clock. It was almost quitting time. What a long fucking day, she thought. She was surviving off sugar and coffee. She needed something substantial.

Want to get some dinner later?

She held her breath as she watched bubbles appear, then disappear, then appear again. Right as she was sending a backpedaling message, Sarah's response popped up.

Sure. Aunt Judy will watch Harley. What's good around here?

Spruce Mountain had three restaurants. Gravy's was a diner that wasn't private or quiet at all. Moby's was a family restaurant, which was a step up from Gravy's. And then there was Mountain View, the only upscale restaurant. It filled up on Valentine's Day and important anniversaries. They could always go to Ophelia's in Sawyer, which was a fifteen-minute drive with a lot more options, but truthfully, Natalie wanted to chill.

We could go to Moby's or I can cook something. She wasn't in the mood to cook, but she didn't want to have to explain why the two of them were out together. Small-town talk was alive and well in Spruce Mountain.

You cook?

Natalie smiled. *Meh. It's passable for food. Any restrictions?*

Nope.

Steaks on the grill and a salad?

Perfect. What time and what's your address?

Shit. Now she was going to have to clean up the place, shower, and start dinner. *Is six thirty too late?*

No. That gives me time to feed Harley and get a few things done, too.

I'll see you then.

Natalie didn't want to leave work early again, so she watched the clock until it struck five and grabbed her coat. "Have a good evening, everyone. Call me if anything happens."

She hoped that tonight, of all nights, the town would be quiet.

CHAPTER SIX

I brought wine and sparkling cider, in case you don't drink wine." Sarah held up two bottles when Natalie opened the door. She tried to maintain eye contact and not openly stare at Natalie. The sheriff's uniform was sexy, but Natalie in tight leggings and an oversized sweater that almost slipped off her shoulder made Sarah's knees weak.

"Come on in. I waited to throw the steaks on the grill because I don't know how you like yours cooked." Natalie stepped back and waited for Sarah to enter.

"You have a very nice place," Sarah said. Natalie's bungalow was located on the edge of town on a full acre. It was decorated very simply but tastefully, with warm colors. She headed straight for the fireplace with her hands held out. "And I can't tell you how much I've missed fireplaces."

"Not a lot of need for them in Texas, huh?" Natalie asked.

"They have them, but they aren't needed as much as they are here. Most of Texas is hot. I know not everybody loves the four seasons, but I love them. Harley's never had a white Christmas," Sarah said. She rubbed her hands together for a few moments and turned back to Natalie. "But I also don't remember Spruce being this cold."

Natalie shrugged. "This cold is unusual for us this time of

year, but I'm sure Harley will see a white Christmas. Unless you move to Portland. Then no. Probably not."

"I really like the idea of opening a business and seeing what happens here. I mean, the town is small, but it has a lot of potential," Sarah said. She heard the huskiness in her own voice and cleared her throat. Natalie's raised eyebrow indicated that she heard it, too. "I brought a Malbec to drink with dinner."

"You might have to open it. I'm really bad with corkscrews." Natalie waved her left hand. "Or just a naturally awkward lefty."

"Is it bad that I'm an expert?" Sarah crinkled her nose playfully and took the bottle from Natalie. Their fingertips brushed during the exchange, and Sarah noticed the gasp that escaped Natalie's lips. As a matter of fact, it boosted Sarah's confidence that maybe, after all these years, there was still something between them.

"Let me find the corkscrew."

Sarah took the moment to fully appreciate Natalie's impressive body when she turned to retrieve the bottle opener. She had her hair pulled up, but several strands hung down, giving it the messy but adorably cute look. "How long have you been in this house?"

"I bought it a few years ago and spent a lot of time and energy remodeling it."

"You did it all yourself?" Sarah stared at Natalie with new appreciation.

"The butch in me got to use all kinds of power tools. It was good because I had a lot of energy to expel after my dad died."

"I'm sorry. I didn't mean to bring up something sad." Sarah took the glass from Natalie's outstretched hand, careful not to touch her for fear of dropping the glass and embarrassing herself.

Natalie waved her off. "I got to spend quality time with my father. I came back because I was needed and stayed because I like being a part of something good. I know that probably sounds corny or weird."

Sarah reached out and gently squeezed Natalie's forearm. "I think it's great. When I was here, I didn't like it because it's a small town, and I felt like I was too big for it. Now that I'm back, I'm starting to understand its charm." She skillfully opened the bottle and poured two glasses of wine at Natalie's nod. "And you have blossomed here." A pink blush brushed across Natalie's neck and cheeks. More courage for Sarah. "You've come a long way since high school."

"We both have," Natalie said.

Sarah felt chills tingle her arms and legs at the smoothness of Natalie's voice. Natalie was so confident and sure. "I'm sorry I wasn't nicer to you in high school."

Natalie crossed her arms and rested her elbows on the counter. That put her comfortably in Sarah's personal space. Sarah always loved how Natalie's eyes reminded her of the dark-blue ocean right before a storm.

"Trust me, you were nicer than most. High school was the worst."

"But look at you now. You're successful, respected, and beautiful." Sarah took a sip of wine to calm her growing nervousness.

"Now I can arrest everyone who's still here who was a jerk in school."

"I love it, but I think you're kidding?"

Sarah laughed when Natalie wiggled her hand side to side, indicating that it was a toss-up.

"Tell me about you. The other night at the bar, we only talked about me and my bad decisions. Except for Harley. She's the best decision I ever made."

"Let me throw the steaks on the grill, and then we can sit and relax, and you can ask me all the questions," Natalie said.

Through the sliding-glass door, Sarah watched Natalie place two thick steaks on the grill, close the lid, and slip back inside. Sarah handed her the glass of wine and sat opposite her, but still in front of the fire.

"Are you dating anyone?" Sarah hated to start off with that straight-to-the-gut question, but she wanted to hear it straight from Natalie and not Judy. Gossip wasn't always right.

"No. I had a girlfriend in Bend for about a year, but it didn't work out."

Sarah bit the inside of her cheeks to keep herself from smiling at the news that Natalie was single and that she had heard it straight from her, not just depended on gossip from the other night. Again, not that she was in any position to start dating so quickly after the divorce, but it was hard not to have tiny fantasies about her. "Distance?"

Natalie nodded. "And we just weren't right for one another. We should have broken up sooner. I let it go too long."

"I get that. Sometimes it's easier to cling to what used to be in a relationship than to deal with the problem straight on." Sarah raised her hand. "I speak from experience."

"Tell me about…Francine, right?" Natalie asked.

"She practices sports medicine down in Fort Worth. She works with the women's soccer team at Texas Christian University."

"You played soccer?"

Sarah snorted out a laugh. "Oh, God, no. Don't you remember how awful I was at high school sports? Francine and I met after I graduated. We were the perfect couple on paper and decided to get married. She didn't want kids, and I thought I could change her mind. I threatened to leave when our relationship hit rock bottom, and should have, but she suggested that we start a family, so I stayed. We had Harley, and I was so happy with a baby I didn't realize she wasn't, and I caught her in not one, but two affairs."

"Ouch. How is Harley adjusting to single-parent life?" Natalie asked.

"Honestly? I don't think she even noticed. I'm not even kidding when I say Francine didn't want kids. That was her way of keeping me."

"Does she communicate with Harley? I don't mean to pry, and you don't even have to answer me." Natalie shook her head.

"It's okay. This is a safe space. You can ask me anything. Francine calls her once a week, but I predict that now that we've moved, those conversations will eventually fade away." Sarah put her wineglass on the table and moved closer to the fire.

"Ack. I'm sorry. That can't be easy for either one of you."

"I'm good. Healed. And I really think Harley is adjusting well. She doesn't seem sad or super excited when Francine calls. She treats her like a family friend."

"I'd like to meet Harley someday. Hang on. I have to check on the steaks." Natalie slipped on a jacket this time and disappeared onto the deck.

Sarah stared at the fire. Everything about this felt right. Spending time with Natalie, being here in her house next to the fireplace. Aside from the millions of butterflies in her stomach that danced every time she saw or thought of Natalie, she was completely at ease. Spruce Mountain was a surprisingly easy adjustment. She had dreaded the drama she thought would be here when she returned, but she'd slipped right back into life as though the last seventeen years had happened in the blink of an eye.

"They're almost ready. Medium, right?" Natalie shrugged out of her jacket and set the table.

"Let me help with something. Anything." Sarah stood but sat when Natalie pointed the salad tongs at her and snapped them together a few times.

"You're my guest, so you stay put."

Sarah shivered at the authoritative yet playful manner Natalie took with her. Her tiny fantasy of kissing Natalie again had turned into a full-blown make-out session as she imagined Natalie taking charge in bed. She shook off the delicious vision and held her hands up in resignation as she waited for Natalie to grab the steaks and put them on the table. "Everything looks wonderful."

"This is an easy meal. I normally don't cook unless I go to my mother's."

"I'm sure it's fantastic. Thank you for inviting me." Sarah pulled out her chair and sat when Natalie did.

"It's good to see you again after all these years."

As sexy as Natalie's mouth was, it was her eyes that stunned Sarah—slightly hooded and flashing with hunger that disappeared, but not before Sarah saw it. She stifled another shiver and cleared her throat. "I honestly didn't know who would still be here after all these years. Small towns don't attract a lot of people." She didn't tell Natalie that she knew she was still in town. Aunt Judy had dropped her name from time to time for reasons that were crystal clear now.

"I'm surprised I stayed."

"Yeah. Why didn't you go back to Denver?"

Natalie held her fingers in front of her mouth until she was done chewing. "I worked a plane wreck, and it was the worst thing I've ever experienced. I had nightmares for weeks. When my mom called and told me about my dad, I didn't hesitate. I quit the force, packed up, and headed to Spruce."

"You've had it rough for a while, huh?" Sarah took a sip of wine and thought about Natalie's hardships over the years. Even though she had just gone through a divorce, and her parents were no longer close enough to visit, they were still alive and available by phone if she needed them. Her life had been pretty normal.

"It was rough there for a bit, but my life has settled down. I like the person I've become, and I really enjoy being sheriff."

"I hear you're really good at it."

Another blush flooded Natalie's cheeks, and Sarah felt something slip inside her. Her heart, which had been locked up and put away for over a year, fluttered briefly. It was as if at this very moment, she finally accepted how perfect Natalie was. No, no, no. She couldn't fall for her. What if she couldn't make enough money in Spruce and had to move? Natalie had been through so much, and Sarah had already hurt her once so many years ago.

"It's not nearly as challenging as Denver, but Spruce surprisingly accepted something new."

"What do you mean?"

Natalie pointed to herself. "A giant lesbian comes in and makes all sorts of changes. I thought for sure I would get chased out of town."

Sarah remembered when people had made fun of Natalie for being so tall in high school and the mean things they had said. She wasn't guilty of saying those words, but she was guilty of not speaking out to protect her. "You're not a giant."

"My whole life I was teased for being different. Being tall and being gay."

After grabbing Natalie's hand on impulse, Sarah squeezed it. "Listen, I'm sorry I didn't defend you in high school, but I always thought you were wonderful. You always looked out for everyone in our class. You took the brunt of the bullying for so many people, and I noticed."

She wasn't sure if she entwined their fingers or if Natalie did it, but either way, adrenaline rushed through her and caused every part of her to be aware of their connection. Her pulse raced, her heart ached, and the soft spot between her thighs throbbed. She had to pull back. She couldn't hurt Natalie again. As strong as Natalie was, she was vulnerable, and Sarah knew it. Not that Natalie was needy, because she wasn't, but Sarah was certain that, if they slept together, Natalie would put all of herself into their fledgling relationship, and Sarah couldn't commit right now. She slowly pulled away, under the guise of wanting a sip of wine.

"For the most part, people accept me. I mean, a few old men in town hate that I'm in charge of things, but I always treat them fairly and tell them to get over it. I mean, who's going to argue with me? A lesbian with a pistol, a stun gun, and a baton?"

A small laugh replaced the retort that Sarah wanted to make. "Well, I've heard only good things, so here's to many more years of being in charge and making the town feel safe." Sarah held out her wineglass and playfully clinked it with Natalie's.

"Do you want to sit by the fire? These chairs aren't comfortable."

Sarah nodded and followed Natalie over to the fireplace. They sat in the same places as before and continued their talk. It was getting late, but Sarah couldn't remember a time when she felt so relaxed and excited at the same time. Aunt Judy had promised Harley would be taken care of and put to bed at a decent time.

"What time do you have to work tomorrow?"

"I'll get in about eight."

"Let me guess, usually earlier?"

There was that genuine smile again. "What can I say?"

"I should probably go then." Sarah stood and gave a little cat-like stretch and handed her now-empty wineglass to Natalie. "Thank you so much for dinner and welcoming me back after all these years." She didn't want to go but didn't want to overstay her welcome.

"Now you know where I live." Natalie followed her over to the coat rack and helped her slip her jacket on. Her fingers brushed gently along the side of Sarah's neck as she folded down the collar and turned her around to face her, her fingers now on either side of the unzipped jacket.

Sarah almost gave a soft moan at Natalie's gentleness and command of something as simple as helping her put on a jacket. "Now I know where you live." Sarah unconsciously licked her lips and looked at Natalie's full ones. Flashback to Ellie's party and Natalie's hand on the back of her neck keeping her firmly in place while she deepened the kiss. "Have a great night." She wanted to feel Natalie's full lips pressed against hers. Wanted to feel her hands slip inside her jacket and pull her close. Instead, she pulled Natalie into a hug, thinking it was the safer route. But feeling Natalie's long legs and her breasts press into her was almost unbearable. She regrettably pulled away and gave her a quick smile before walking out the door.

She had no idea how she was able to get to her car without her knees buckling. She waved and slowly backed down the driveway, appreciating Natalie's form silhouetted in her doorway. Sarah knew she was in trouble when she pulled into Aunt Judy's driveway and her legs were still shaking. She put her head on the steering wheel and groaned. This time she didn't have the luxury of leaving like she did seventeen years ago, when her heart had raced just this fast and just as furiously.

CHAPTER SEVEN

W e haven't heard anything about Ghost Dog in a few days, Sheriff. Maybe he finally found his home." Faith handed Natalie purchase orders to sign as soon as she walked through the door.

"Hopefully so." Natalie ignored the hollow feeling in her chest. It wasn't as if she'd known this dog for more than a few moments last week, but something made her sad. It was the unknown. Was he lost? Still in the woods? Hungry? Cold? Or had he found his way home? She showed no emotion when she signed the documents and gave them back to Faith. "Anything else going on? And where's Betty?"

She nodded. "Betty's over at the school. Cracked window was reported. Could have been kids or a tree branch. The wind was a bit crazy last night."

Everything was crazy last night, Natalie thought. She hung up her jacket and hat and walked into her office. Regardless of what she thought or Sarah thought, last night was a date. They had been subtly flirting, like the way Sarah had lowered her eyes when they talked about the past, or how she always reached out and touched Natalie's arm. Oh, and don't even get her started on the hug. The one that lasted far longer than a friendship hug? And what about the small moan Sarah had made when she gathered her coat in her fists and turned her around? She'd almost kissed her then. Almost.

If Sarah planned to stay in Spruce Mountain long term, and if she hadn't had to get home to Harley, Natalie would have kissed her. Not that fumbling first kiss that was still perfect, but the kind where she lifted Sarah into her arms and leaned her up against the door. The kind where Sarah automatically wrapped her legs around Natalie's waist so both of them could find some friction for relief. Sarah would have welcomed at least a kiss, but now wasn't the time. Natalie refused to be the rebound girl no matter how much she wanted to sleep with Sarah. She couldn't go through the angst of watching her leave again.

"Hey, Boss." Faith belted out the words so everyone could hear. Just the two of them were in the station, but her receptionist wasn't even trying to be professional and use the phone. "When are you bringing in the trailer for the pumpkin festival? I'm going to need some time to decorate it."

Natalie pressed her fingers against her eyelids to relieve some of the burning she felt there from lack of sleep. Fuck. She'd forgotten about digging out the wagon from her oversized shed. It was going to take her at least thirty minutes of moving things around just to free it. She took a deep breath and picked up the phone. "Yes. I'll get it before this weekend."

"Great. I can decorate it with things from Mom's store. I'll call her in a bit and tell her to pull some things together."

It was hard to grasp that loud and obnoxious Faith was related to sweet and quiet Greta Bowman of Creative Crafts. Natalie pinched the bridge of her nose and thought about everything she would have to do just to unload the boxes and boxes of stuff that were piled high in her shed on top of the wagon. At least the sun was shining today. And the temperature was warmer than yesterday. Maybe she would do it on her lunch break.

Obviously, Faith wanted and needed something to do. "Okay, okay. You'll need time to decorate it. I'll get it after lunch."

Natalie hung up to Faith's squeals of delight. She didn't need to be on the phone to hear her shouts of approval. The impending headache that had started throbbing was going to make an appearance any moment. She needed caffeine. The smell of freshly brewed coffee made her grab her cup and head into the small kitchen. "Doughnuts? Where did you get doughnuts?"

"Over in Lexington. I bought them on my way in."

Faith's singsongy voice could only mean one thing. She got laid last night. For some reason, Faith always wanted to confide in Natalie when it came to relationships or sex, even though Betty was far more qualified and definitely more interested in listening. Natalie dug up two aspirin and grabbed a doughnut before braving her way back into the common area, where Faith was already banging on her keyboard.

Upon closer inspection, she saw that Faith was working and not shopping online. "Look at this." She pointed to the monitor. Natalie followed her finger and saw a post on their public board.

"What's the date on it?" Natalie asked.

They both hunched over the monitor and watched a home-security video of Ghost Dog from two nights ago. He was sniffing the ground and was only on video for about ten seconds, but it gave Natalie hope. She was happy he was still alive and not lost in the woods or hit by a car.

"I think I'll patrol for him. Call me if you need me." She took two big bites of the doughnut and left the remaining half hanging out of her mouth as she swung on her jacket and grabbed the keys. "Hell Hetty to hall he."

"Tell Betty to call you. Will do," Faith said. She returned to her monitor and waved as Natalie turned and used her hip to open the front door.

The dog was still in her county. Somewhere, somehow, he was surviving. The post was from Bradford's ranch. That made total sense. Most of the livestock were sheep and lambs. Ghost Dog could easily slip in and be warm and find food there. She drove slowly through town, waved at the kids on their way to school, and stopped to talk to Phil Murphy, who was hoisting the American flag at the post office. She lowered the window and waved him over.

"Good morning, Phil. You haven't seen a golden retriever out and about, have you?"

"No, ma'am. I heard you were looking for one. Is it yours?"

Phil's voice was clipped and professional. He took his job as postmaster very seriously and always ran a tight ship. Most workers didn't last long because Spruce Mountain was a place people passed through, not put down roots. Phil knew that, but it still pissed him off, and he liked to complain about it to Natalie at every opportunity.

"He's not, but he belongs to a friend of mine." As much as Natalie hated lying, personalizing the dog would make people less likely to shoot it. "I'm headed up to Bradford's place. They posted a video of him on their property."

Phil nodded for about five seconds, wished her good luck, and tapped the patrol car on the hood with his large hand, which only made Natalie's headache worse. She raised the window and pulled back out onto Main Street, slowly, abiding by the twenty-mile-an-hour posted sign. It gave her time to glance down cross streets to see if Ghost Dog was around.

The ranch was about five miles out of town, and Natalie always loved visiting. Nothing could get her hat off and on her knees faster than playing with baby lambs. The Bradfords had an area open to the public, where they could feed the baby animals, and it was a surprisingly popular tourist attraction. Tourists brought money to Spruce Mountain, and businesses boomed during the summer when people would head for the mountains to get away for the weekends. Everyone stopped at the ranch, then picked up souvenirs in town. Playing with baby animals released endorphins, and visitors were more inclined to buy the cutesy crafts on display outside of Creative Crafts or the general store. Even Chuck's Chainsaw Cuts saw a significant boost during the summer. Natalie wondered what people did with the oversized chainsaw wooden sculptures they bought. She couldn't even pretend to like them.

Dustin, whom Natalie used to babysit, was riding his horse along the fence line of the ranch. "Dustin, how are you?"

"Hey, Sheriff. I'm good. Just doing a daily check. What brings you out here?" He politely took off his hat and played with the brim of it while Natalie explained her purpose. "Oh, yeah. I sent that video in. Is that your dog? He sure is big."

How Dustin sounded Southern way up in the mountains of Oregon blew Natalie's mind. Even when he was a kid, he sounded like he was from Texas.

"He's a friend's dog. And he's not very easy to find or catch. We thought we had him cornered under a house, but we caught a ten-pound marmot instead." Fuck, now she was picking up the slow accent. She cleared her throat and enunciated every word properly and clearly. "Do you mind if I take a look around? "Translation. Can I walk around and then maybe slip into the barn to see the lambs?"

"Sure. Go ahead and park up by the big barn, and I'll meet

you up there in a few minutes." He put his hat back on and waited for Natalie to pass.

She drove slowly to not kick up any dust from the gravel. The ranch was impressive in size and functionality. The Bradfords were well known in the area. The property, which had doubled in size since Natalie had first gotten to know the family, had been purchased several generations ago during the mass migration west for gold.

She parked and slid out from behind the wheel and waited for Dustin, who was only a minute or two behind her.

"I haven't seen the dog other than on video, but there's a lot of ground to cover. I can look through the trail cameras and see if I find anything. Usually we spot coyotes, foxes, deer, and raccoons. I'll have them comb through the cameras." Dustin slid off his horse and tethered it to the railing outside the barn. "Now, for official sheriff business, I'm going to need your help with something."

For a moment, Natalie thought he was serious, until she followed him into the barn, where he directed her into a small stall where two tiny lambs huddled together under a heat lamp.

Natalie cooed at their cuteness and squatted down with Dustin. "Can I touch them?"

He plucked one up from the warm hay. "Sure. Their mama has milk fever, so we've been bottle-feeding these two. They'll go into rotation for the petting zoo once they're old enough. They're used to being handled by people." He put the lamb in her arms and picked up the other one so it wouldn't get cold.

Natalie nuzzled the soft fuzz of the lamb's face. "Oh, my goodness. How do you get any work done around here with this much cuteness?" She giggled when the lamb tried to eat her hair.

"Feeding time. Ready to help?"

She nodded and followed Dustin over to the feeding area, where another ranch hand was feeding two goats. "Are you putting them in the wagon Saturday? I vote yes."

"They're almost too little, but if I get enough volunteers, I will. I need to make sure they stay warm. Usually we welcome new babies in the winter. These two are pretty special. After we feed them, I'll show you our wagon. Are you having one this year?"

Natalie nodded. "I don't know why, but Faith insists. At least people aren't scared of us anymore."

"I don't know that I'd go that far. Here. You know what to do." He handed Natalie a warm bottle and pointed her in the direction of a hay bale.

"Official law-enforcement business, huh? I'll take it." The lamb wasted no time finding the bottle and tugged on the nipple. "Whoa, there, little girl. There's plenty here for you." She laughed at the greedy lamb's lips and stroked her coat as she drank. "She's so soft. How can you stand to be away from them?"

"Mom usually does the feedings, but today she's out and asked me to. You got lucky."

"I sure did. Your wagon always does well on Super Saturday."

Spruce Mountain closed down Main Street the day before Halloween, and the businesses lined the streets with wagons of merchandise to sell or give away. Bradford Ranch always had goat cheese, milk, and samples of wool. It was the busiest wagon because of the baby animals. Natalie was a sucker. She thought about Sarah and how Harley, a six-year-old she'd never met, would love it. She pulled out her phone and snapped a quick selfie of her with the lamb and sent it to Sarah. Her phone dinged before she even put it back in her pocket.

I swear you have the best job in town. Totally and completely JEALOUS.

Being the sheriff is hard work. She gave a stern look at the camera and sent another photo.

Where are you? And why am I not with you?

Natalie called Sarah. "It's very hard to text and feed a hungry lamb."

"Hi." Sarah's voice sounded warm and delicious, like she just woke up. "Tell me why a sheriff is feeding a baby lamb."

"I stand by my claim of official law-enforcement business. I'm following up a lead on Ghost Dog. The Bradfords had video from a few nights ago that showed the stray dog. I thought maybe he was still here."

"You still haven't found him? That makes me so sad," Sarah said.

Natalie's heart dropped. "He's so sweet. I really want to find him and his home. Hopefully he's chipped. I don't remember him having a collar." She was jarred back to the conversation when the lamb bleated out her frustration at not getting more milk out of the bottle.

Dustin reached over and held it at an angle. "Like this. Don't piss her off."

"I just got in trouble." Natalie giggled into the phone, knowing full well Sarah heard the lamb and Dustin scolding her.

"Do you need to get off the phone?"

The comfort level Natalie had with Sarah gave her a warmth that spread from her heart outward. "Nope. I'm a professional. I've got this. Listen, this Saturday, Main Street shuts down, and the shops open early or have wagons where you can shop or get free stuff. I think you and Harley should go. Then you can bottle-feed lambs or goats." Natalie tried to keep the excitement of seeing Sarah again out of her voice.

"The weather is supposed to be nice this weekend. I think we can make it."

"Our department's wagon is boring, but we do have candy for the kids. And my mom bakes cookies and brownies. I swear that's the reason I got reelected."

Sarah laughed. "Because of your mom's baking?"

"It's phenom. Anyway, I need to go and finish up my official business. I'll talk to you later."

"Thanks for calling, Nat. It was a nice surprise."

When Natalie hung up, her smile couldn't have been any bigger.

❖

For a second, Natalie considered showering before digging into the shed to haul out the wagon. She was covered in dust, dirt, hay, and milky lamb slobber. Now that she was away from the ranch, the smell that lingered on her uniform wasn't great. But knowing she would get dirty moving things around, she kept on her uniform and decided the shower could wait until after the wagon was freed. She reached up and clicked on her walkie. "This is Sheriff Strand. No luck at Bradfords. I'm retrieving the wagon now. I should be back to the office by two." That gave her enough time to take a quick shower and eat lunch.

"Okay, Sheriff. I'll call if anything comes up."

Natalie opened the door and flipped on the light. Then she put her hands on her hips and sighed. This was going to take a while to unload. Thankfully her Jeep was out in the driveway, so she could move stacks of boxes to that side of the shed, where it usually was parked. The squad car got the garage. After dropping the third box, she heard a scuffling noise in the back that made her pause. Visions of a giant marmot ready to attack filled her overactive imagination. She grabbed her baton and circled the wagon. Instead of finding an R.O.U.S., there, on a padded blanket, sat Ghost Dog.

"What are you doing here? We've been looking for you for a long time." She slowly walked to him and squatted so she could be at eye level and not frighten him. "Have you been here this whole time?" He wagged his tail and kissed her hand. She felt his neck for a collar as she stroked his fur. "Are you hungry, boy? Do you want to go inside and warm up?"

She carefully stood and looked for something she could use as a leash to get him from the shed into the house. "How do I not have any rope in this entire place?" Fishing line was too thin. She ended up cutting off a piece of an old Thanksgiving vinyl tablecloth that was padded on one side and made a short leash about two inches wide and six feet long. By the time she adjusted it for his neck, the lead was only three feet long. "Let's go inside, okay?"

Natalie made her voice sweet and calm. Ghost Dog wagged his tail. She held the end of the makeshift leash tight and opened the door. He walked calmly beside her, up the porch stairs, and into her house as if he belonged there. She carefully removed the leash and let him get comfortable. He never left her side.

"How about scrambled eggs? With some cheese? Does that sound good?" He wagged his tail again. Natalie found a deep bowl and poured some water into it and put it next to the refrigerator. He walked over to it when she moved away and lapped up about half of it.

She shot a text off to Faith: *I have Ghost Dog. He was in my shed next to the trailer. I'm going to figure things out with him before I return. Radio silence. Text or call me if something comes up. He seems to be spooked by loud noises.*

No way! Do you need help?

No. We're good. Thanks though.

Natalie turned off her walkie and patted her leg. The dog approached her slowly, tail wagging, nose down low. She stroked his back softly and whispered encouraging words. "You're such a good boy. Why do you always run away from us? Did somebody bad hurt you?" She moved slowly and pulled out ingredients for scrambled eggs. He kept his distance and licked his chops from time to time as Natalie fixed them both lunch.

She looked into his soulful eyes and told him he was going to have to wait a few minutes for the eggs to cool. She sprinkled cheese on top, more for herself than for him, and salted hers to taste. He got the bigger portion and a piece of unbuttered toast. When she put his plate down, he looked up at her as if waiting for permission. "It's okay. Go ahead and eat." She stood as she watched him wolf down all the eggs and the toast.

She picked up his cleaned plate and wondered if it was enough for him. How much food did a seventy-pound dog need? He was thin, but she didn't think he was malnourished. She was going to have to take him to Dr. Wallace and check to see if he was chipped, what she needed to feed him, and how they could find his fur parents.

"Sheriff Strand." Her eyes were on Ghost Dog, not caller ID.

"Nat. Hi. It's Sarah."

Natalie fumbled the phone in surprise but secured it before it clattered on the counter. "Sarah, hi. What's up?" She paced the kitchen until Ghost Dog started following her.

"Aunt Judy wants to know if you and your mom want to meet us for drinks again Friday at Tanner's. I know you're probably too busy Friday night with the pumpkin festival on Saturday."

Natalie tapped her fingers on the counter while staring at the dog, wondering if she should agree to go. Would she still have the dog, or would she find his owner by then? "Okay. My answer is yes, but I don't know for how long. Guess who's in my kitchen?" She didn't wait for Sarah to answer. "The lost dog. He was living in my shed."

"What? This whole time?"

"I don't know. I'm still trying to figure how he got in because he's not exactly small." Natalie sat down on the floor next to Ghost Dog and petted his chest while she tried to figure out what to do with him. "He's adorable, Sarah."

"If you need to stay at home with him, I get it. I'll see you Saturday. Aunt Judy said they have a pumpkin-painting contest that I want to take Harley to, so we'll be down there," Sarah said.

"Can I give you an answer Friday? I want to try to find this fella's home. Somebody has to be missing him." She made a list of everything she needed, including a brush, a leash, a chew toy, and appropriate dog food. She plucked a few pieces of hay from his thick fur and smoothed down his reddish-gold coat.

"Maybe you can bring him to the festival if you haven't found his home?"

"I don't know. He's very skittish. Plus, a lot of people have been scolding him around town, so he probably has mixed feelings about them, you know?"

"I get it. Just keep me posted. I'm sure I'll find you. Spruce Mountain isn't that big."

"Plus, I have your number."

"Just don't be afraid to use it."

CHAPTER EIGHT

S he said she'd be there. Are you sure you can't make it?"
Sarah stared at Aunt Judy, who lay under the covers with a
cold compress on her forehead.

"This headache is wicked. Just go ahead and apologize
to the ladies. We can try it again next week. I want to get rid
of this headache before tomorrow so I can have fun at the
festival." Judy waved her off and groaned when she turned
her head.

"Okay. Take care. I'll tell Harley to keep it down tonight.
I'm sure she and Uncle Bob will just watch *Frozen* or put a
puzzle together." Sarah felt guilty leaving while her aunt had
a headache, but the Strands were expecting them, and she
didn't want to disappoint Natalie. Who was she kidding? She
couldn't wait to see Natalie again.

She finished primping, but not without overthinking her
makeup. Less eye shadow and more mascara, or more eye
shadow and less mascara? Should she put on lipstick? She
straightened her hair and flattened her sweater. It was tighter
than what she normally wore, but she liked how it flattered
her figure. She sighed and reminded herself it wasn't a date—
just three friends getting together for drinks. Tanner's was
probably going to be packed. Aunt Judy told her to get there

early, because a lot of people would be out celebrating the night before Spruce Mountain's Super Saturday.

"Don't stay up late," Sarah said. She kissed and hugged Harley before tucking her back under the blanket on the couch.

"It's the weekend, Mom. Can I wait up for you?"

Sarah knew Harley wouldn't last past nine, so she upped her bedtime to eight thirty. "No arguments. And water only to drink." That was directed more toward Uncle Bob, who raised his hands in self-defense.

"We'll try to get her tucked in by then, and we definitely won't have popcorn and apple juice. Definitely won't." He gave Harley an exaggerated wink. She promptly fell into a fit of giggles by his side.

Sarah shook her head. "Good night, and keep the noise level down. Aunt Judy has a bad headache." She waved on her way out the door and closed it softly. For a moment, she thought about walking to the bar, to cool off her warm thoughts of Natalie, but she already knew that being that close to her would have her burning all night. For as much as she was fighting the attraction, she sure was making herself available to her.

The bar was already crowded when Sarah arrived. She parked down a side street and had to walk a block. No way would they get a quiet booth like last time. Smiling at the nice guy who held the door open, Sarah snaked her way through a small cluster of people right by the door and looked around.

"Over here, Sarah."

Natalie's voice was unmistakable. Commandingly smooth, it rose above the crowd. Sarah turned and found her in the last booth near the pool table.

"You scored valuable real estate here." Sarah sat across from Natalie and shrugged off her coat.

"That's because I'm the sheriff." Natalie winked at her.

Sarah smiled and looked away. Natalie was too fucking charming. "Where's your mom?"

"She was under the weather. Where's Judy?"

Sarah sat up straight in the booth and crossed her arms. "Funny how my aunt suddenly developed a headache right before it was time to leave."

Natalie leaned forward to hear better. "I think they're in cahoots."

Sarah tried not to stare at the smooth skin above the vee of Natalie's sweater or focus on the pink lace bra that peeked out right at her collarbone. She leaned closer, not only to get a better look, but to hear her better. "What should we do with them?"

The intensity of Natalie's stare made Sarah shiver. "Thank them," she said. "I'm going to need a drink."

Natalie nodded and waved Trinity over.

"I'll have a gin and tonic with a splash of lime," Sarah said.

"Good choice." Natalie held up her half-empty glass, showing Sarah it was her drink of choice for the evening, too.

"Scoot over. I can't hear you from here," Sarah said. The bar was ten times louder tonight than the last time they were there. She knew she should keep her distance. Natalie had somehow taken over most of her waking thoughts and all her dreams, and now she was purposely getting closer under the guise of not being able to hear her.

Natalie shifted to her side of the table. "Is this better?"

She was smirking as if she knew the effect she had on Sarah. Seventeen years ago, she'd been this close to Natalie under different circumstances. Her heart pounded with the same intensity and need as it had that night. She swallowed hard when her mouth went dry because she was just staring at the blueness of Natalie's eyes and the redness of her lips. God, she had great lips. The shy girl so many years ago really knew how to kiss. But how? She had never seen Natalie with anyone in high school. "I can hear you better, if that's what you mean."

"Okay. We can start with that."

Talking wasn't really an option with her tongue tied and her stomach in knots. There was no mistaking it. Natalie was interested in her. If Trinity hadn't shown up with her drink right then, Sarah would have done or said something stupid. She took a large swallow, grimaced, and hissed through her clenched teeth. "I think they forgot the tonic." The straight alcohol pinched her sinuses, and she stifled a cough that burned in her throat.

"Here. Have a sip of my water."

Sarah gratefully took the glass and drank half in a matter of seconds. She nodded at Natalie and put her hand against her throat. "Thank you. That helped."

"Well, since our family ditched us and the people here are entirely too loud, do you want to go somewhere a little quieter?"

That suggestion piqued a little more than just Sarah's interest. "What do you have in mind?" Sarah watched Natalie play with the condensation on the glass.

"We could always go back to my place. That would give me a chance to check on Ghost Dog, and you could meet him. And I promise I'll add tonic to your gin."

Sarah cocked her head. "Should I trust you?"

Natalie scooted closer. "The real question is, should I trust you?"

Sarah opened her mouth and then clamped it shut. Was that a reference to Ellie's party? "Uh, I think so? I mean, I'm pretty innocent."

"Pretty innocent?" Natalie winked. "Come on. Let's get out of here. This place is giving me a headache."

Sarah slid out of the booth and waited for Natalie to put on her coat. "I'll follow you." They moved, and a group of four somewhat rowdy young adults swooped in to take their booth, almost trampling Sarah in the process. Natalie turned and waited until she had their attention.

"I'd better not hear about anybody here driving after drinking all this alcohol. I have a nice night ahead of me and an early morning tomorrow. The last thing I need is to be called away. Who's driving?"

Four fingers pointed to a young man who stood at the bar ordering a pitcher.

"Zane. Zane, come here." Natalie waved him over. She put her hand on his shoulder. "I heard you are responsible for the table. I want you to tell me you aren't drinking and will make sure everyone gets home safely."

"Sheriff, I only had one beer. I promise I will finish this one and switch to water."

"I need to hear the words, Zane."

Sarah noticed he had a hard time keeping eye contact with Natalie. It was fun to watch their exchange. Although playful, it contained a definite underlying warning.

"I'll make sure everyone gets home safely."

"Thank you. I'll see you all tomorrow at the festival," Natalie said.

Sarah welcomed the cool, crisp air on her heated cheeks. She'd been in the bar only fifteen minutes, but being close to Natalie was raising her body temperature to an uncomfortable level. She kept her jacket unzipped and walked a few steps from the entrance, then waited for Natalie to catch up.

"Want to follow me?"

"Sure. I know the way."

❖

"Oh, my gosh. This is the escape bandit?" Sarah fell to her knees and dug her fingers into the golden's fur. She nuzzled his face and kissed his ear. "He's gorgeous."

"Yeah. He's the rabid beast the town's been talking about. Hey, buddy. You doing okay? You need to go outside?"

Sarah stood and watched as Natalie hooked him up to a leash and promised they would be back in a flash.

"Make yourself at home. Gin's in the bar by the fireplace, and fresh limes are in the refrigerator."

Ten minutes later, when Natalie returned with Ghost Dog, Sarah greeted her with a gin and tonic garnished with a fresh lime wedge. "I thought I would leave the fire up to you because I have zippo experience with lighting them, and I didn't want to burn down this beautiful house. Not after all the hard work you've put into it."

"That was really thoughtful. As long as the flue is open, you shouldn't have a problem. I'll get one started."

Natalie took a sip of the drink and lifted her eyebrows in surprise. "If the library thing doesn't pan out, you can be a bartender at Tanner's."

"Thank you, but the hours suck. I could never do anything in the evenings."

"Oh, like go on a date?"

The heat she'd just left at the bar flashed across her body. She avoided Natalie's eyes but couldn't help a flush from creeping up her neck and landing on her cheeks. "Right. Or tuck Harley in at night or watch movies with her."

"All the important things. I say stick with the library and do taxes on the side. Have you looked into that any more?"

"No, but I need to. My bank account isn't getting any fatter."

Natalie nodded. "I totally get it."

Sarah petted Ghost Dog while Natalie started a fire. "So, where did you come from?" She moved closer to the dog. "You picked a great place to end up. I know Nat will do everything to make sure you find your forever home."

"Are you talking about me? Telling one another secrets?" Natalie pointed the poker at them playfully.

Sarah held her hands up. "Only good things, I promise."

"Come on over. Sit with me." Natalie sat on the couch and patted the empty cushion next to her.

"What were we talking about at the bar?" Sarah sat with plenty of space between them and shifted her position so she was looking at Natalie with the warmth of the fire on her back. She shrugged and shivered at the warmth. "Wherever I end up in this life, I will have to have a fireplace."

"What happens if you go back to Texas?"

Sarah rolled her eyes. "No, thank you. I'm done with the South. Nothing there for me except the past."

"How are you and your ex?"

Sarah took a deep breath. "We're friendly because of Harley, but honestly, I would be happy never talking to her again. I don't wish her any ill will. I just don't care anymore. And I know it sounds bad because she's not a bad person. She just wanted different things from the ones I care about."

"People grow apart. I get that. Tell me more about you. You love your daughter. You're an accountant, and you like all flowers, but specifically lilies."

Sarah laughed. "I like lilies? How do you even know that?"

It was a nice change to see Natalie blush. She took a sip of her drink and cleared her throat. "Ah, I remember a few things from high school. I've always associated you with flowers."

"I do like them a lot. I have three tattoos of lilies."

"You have tattoos?"

"Doesn't everyone anymore?" Sarah asked.

"I don't."

"What? Are you serious?"

Natalie nodded. "No ink on this body. Where are your tats? And can you show them to me?"

Sarah raised her sleeve and pointed to a small tattoo on the inside of her forearm. "I have this one here." She bit her lip when Natalie leaned closer and traced it with her finger. Her touch was warm and soft and made Sarah's eyes flutter shut for half a second. When was the last time she had felt a woman's touch? "I have one on my bikini line and one on my shoulder."

"Turn around."

Sarah almost moaned at Natalie's low, commanding voice. "What?"

Natalie held her forefinger in front of Sarah and made a circular motion with it. "Turn around. I want to see the one on your shoulder."

Sarah slowly turned and pulled down the sleeve of her sweater to reveal the back of her bare shoulder. She felt Natalie's fingers run along the edge of her skin right above the sweater and had to bite her lip again to keep from making a sound.

"It's beautiful. Did this one hurt?"

"More than the other two." Sarah didn't even recognize her own voice. Natalie outlining her tattoo again and again was too much. She scooted away and pulled her sleeve back up over her shoulder. And when she turned around, she didn't realize Natalie was so close. Her eyes dropped to Natalie's mouth and back up to her dark-blue eyes. "It's amazing I don't have more." She pulled away just a little to try to break the control Natalie had over her in that moment, but it was no use. She couldn't stop. She was tired of fighting the "should she or shouldn't she" struggle that raged inside her. "I owe you an apology, Nat."

Natalie leaned back, breaking the spell. "For what?"

"That night. At Ellie's party. Right before I left Spruce Mountain."

Natalie waved her off like she didn't care, but Sarah saw a flash of pain or anger or both cross her features. It was brief, but it packed a punch that Sarah felt deep in the pit of her stomach. She automatically reached out and grabbed Natalie's hand. "I know you remember, because I can't forget it. I blew you off because I wasn't ready to accept who I was back then. I'm sorry I hurt you. I've regretted it every day." She reined in her words for fear of puking out feelings she was still sorting through and scaring the shit out of both of them.

"It's okay. It was a long time ago. We both had some growing up to do."

"It was so rude of me. Do you forgive me?"

"Yes, Sarah. I barely remember. We were kids. It's okay."

Having Natalie accept her apology was a weight off her chest and her heart. "Thank you." It also opened a flood of questions that Sarah really wanted answers to, but she kept her part of the conversation vague and calm. "I always wondered what happened to you and if you were happy."

"Life never goes as planned. My dad's death hit me hard, but I've been fortunate overall. My mom and I have never been closer, and I have a great job. Both keep me pretty busy."

It wasn't the answer Sarah wanted, but she didn't press.

She was afraid of the answer, afraid that maybe her rejection had marred Natalie somehow. Not in an egotistical way, because she didn't think she was anyone special. But in the tender way of when you first fall in love and don't know how high the ceiling is. When your heart is suddenly ripped out from inside your chest when love falls apart. Not that she was in love with Natalie or vice versa, but something had been there between them seventeen years ago, and something was there now. They had unfinished business.

"Tell me about your heart. I feel like you know so much about mine, and I know nothing about yours except that a year ago you dated somebody in Bend." Sarah grabbed her drink and played with the glass to keep her hands busy.

Natalie fell back against the couch and finished her drink. "I wish I had some super-romantic story to tell you, but I don't." She shrugged. "I knew I was gay in high school, experimented in college, and had my first long relationship after college. She was a fitness instructor, and when I came home to help my mom with my dad, she stayed in Denver."

"So, wait a minute. You, a tall, gorgeous, sexy blonde who commands attention when she enters any room, haven't had a solid relationship in eight years except for some woman in Bend? You expect me to believe that?"

"Okay. Maybe there were a few more. It's not as if Spruce Mountain and surrounding towns have a large gay population. I did date the vet here, which ended in disaster."

Sarah loved Natalie's smile. "Okay. Now I have to hear the story. Are you taking Ghost Dog to her?"

"Already did. He's not chipped. Let's just say it was a very quick visit."

Sarah winced. "Do I even want to know what happened there?"

"Several misunderstandings, until I simply gave up trying to explain my job or myself," Natalie said.

She opened up about the complicated relationship and a few others that made Sarah angry at how the previous girlfriends had treated Natalie. "She sounded bitchy, or she wanted way too much from you" alternated after every ex-girlfriend story—a total of six—was revealed to Sarah.

"It's got to be me. I'm the common denominator. I'm just not somebody women date."

Her tone didn't suggest she was asking for pity, and she didn't make excuses. Natalie hadn't given up. She'd just stopped looking. That gave Sarah hope. She couldn't deny that she was attracted to her. "I doubt that. You're perfect, and your person is out there. I just know it."

It was so quiet after she spoke, for a flash she thought she'd gone too far. Maybe she'd revealed too much about what she wanted or touched on what Natalie needed. "And as much as I hate to say this, I think I should probably go. We both have an early start to our day. Mine just happens to be in the form of a highly energetic child, who will no doubt wake me up in six hours." Sarah looked at her watch and stood.

"Ah, the proverbial turning-into-a-pumpkin-at-midnight. Okay, Cinderella. I'll see you in the morning."

Sarah sighed when Natalie took her hand and gently led her to the front door. Ghost Dog followed, nudging his nose against Sarah's hand until she stopped and said good-bye to him. "I won't see you tomorrow, but I'll see you soon. Hopefully on a leash with Sheriff Natalie." She stood and slipped into her jacket that Natalie held open for her.

"Drive carefully. The crazies are out at midnight."

Natalie was so close to her. A calm washed over Sarah as she pulled Natalie into a warm, more-than-friends hug.

She knew what she was going to do. Instead of stressing and overthinking it, she did what she did seventeen years ago, and what she should have done a week ago, and last night. Instead of breaking apart after their good-night hug, she kept her face close to Natalie's and did what she had been dreaming of doing again for so long. She kissed her.

CHAPTER NINE

Natalie lost all concept of time when she felt Sarah's lips press against hers, softly at first. Her memory took her back to that first perfect kiss, and for a moment she thought she was at Ellie's party, except the woman kissing her now was bold and not fueled by cheap alcohol. This woman knew exactly how to kiss.

Sarah's warm body with all her delicious curves brought her back to the present. They were really kissing. Slowing down or breaking apart wasn't even an option. Natalie was trying to figure out how to get closer, even though their bodies were flush. She slipped her hands inside Sarah's coat and ran her fingers along the hem of her sweater, slipping them underneath to stroke the soft skin of her lower back. They both moaned at the contact.

This was the moment she had dreamed of for so many years, and it was worth the wait. She sucked Sarah's bottom lip into her mouth and slipped her tongue inside when Sarah parted her lips. It was heavenly. Just when she didn't think their first kiss could be topped, they perfected it. When she felt Sarah tremble in her arms, Natalie pulled away. She took a deep breath and rested her forehead against Sarah's.

"That just happened, right?"

She felt Sarah pull away too, only to look into her eyes and nod. "Wow. Yes. That just happened." She was breathless and sexy as hell.

"And we are in my house, not Ellie's, right?" Natalie turned her head and saw Ghost Dog a few feet away. "Yes, my house, because there's a dog." Sarah's arms circled her waist and warm lips pressed against her collarbone. She closed her eyes and tilted her head up to afford Sarah more room. When was the last time she felt this much all at once? Passion, need, want, desire, and wetness. The throbbing between her legs was instantaneous. All from a kiss.

"Definitely not at Ellie's house." Sarah took a step back and let out a deep breath. "Okay. I really need to go."

Natalie couldn't let her go. Not now. Not after waiting and wanting for so long. She pulled Sarah back into her arms. "Not yet." She kissed Sarah again, hungry for her taste. It was as if nothing had changed, but everything was a million times better. She moaned when Sarah threaded her fingers through her hair and pressed up against her again.

It took everything she had to keep from lifting Sarah into her arms, wrapping her legs around her waist, and carrying her back to her bedroom to do everything she had fantasized about for years. She slowed the kiss until it was a gentle brush of her lips over Sarah's. "Okay, okay. You have to go. I know."

Sarah let out a shaky laugh. "I hate that I do, but it's probably for the best."

"Here. I'll walk you to your car." Natalie grabbed her coat but stopped when she felt Sarah's hand on her arm.

"I need to separate right now before we both do something crazy. Plus, I need to get home to Harley."

Not that she had anything against Sarah's daughter, but mentioning her gave Natalie pause. "You're right. I'll see you tomorrow morning. Try to get some sleep." She placed a soft kiss on Sarah's slightly swollen lips. "Good night."

"Definitely good night."

Natalie closed the door and leaned against it. What had just happened? One minute they were having a nice conversation, and the next they were in each other's arms trying to get as close as possible. She had wanted Sarah to kiss her but just didn't think she would. When they'd talked about their exes, and even about Ellie's party, Sarah hadn't acted as if she was still interested. That was a long time ago, and even though they had flirted some, Natalie still didn't expect the kiss. She smiled at Ghost Dog. "Let's go for a walk. I have a ton of energy I need to expel." He wagged his tail as if he understood everything.

The twenty-minute walk did nothing to cool her. Ghost Dog seemed happy enough walking the neighborhood as if he belonged there. He pulled her along the same path, smelling the same bushes and marking the same trees. It was strange to be out at night so late, but the town was relatively quiet, and Natalie welcomed the peace. She knew she needed sleep, but she had too much electricity in her veins to even consider sleeping. It was ridiculous really. She was an adult and had been kissed several times in her life. But this was Sarah. The girl who had stolen her heart years ago had suddenly swooped back in and picked up where she left off.

"Buddy, I'm getting nowhere here in my mind. Let's go home." Another tail wag. She opened the door, and he walked over to the fireplace and curled up in his bed. When Natalie had made her list of supplies, a giant fluffy, gray dog bed wasn't on it, but how could she pass up something that looked so perfect for him? He knew what it was the minute she placed it by the bricks. "Get some sleep, buddy. I'll see you in the morning."

❖

Natalie groaned when she heard the alarm. How was it already six in the morning when she'd just gotten to sleep? She was warm, almost hot, and for some reason, she couldn't move her arm. And what was that smell? She cracked open an eyelid. Ghost Dog was snuggled up next to her. As adorable as he was with his head in the crook of her arm and his beautiful brown eyes staring at her, she grimaced. "Buddy, we're going to have to give you a bath if you plan to sneak into my room at night." She hit her alarm and scratched his head. "Come on. Let's get this day started."

Ghost Dog jumped off the bed and woofed at her. She slipped on sweats and slippers and shrugged into a sweatshirt. After a very quick three-minute walk around the yard, Natalie fed him breakfast and filled the tub. She gave a quick whistle. A happy dog entered until he realized what was about to happen. He flattened his ears and very slowly backed out of the bathroom. "Stop being a baby. You need a bath, and we don't have a lot of time. Come on. I'll be gentle. I promise."

Twenty minutes later, huffing like she'd just run five miles, Natalie had Ghost Dog out of the tub and towel dried. As she brushed the tangles out of his hair, she wondered about where he came from and why he chose her. She wasn't a dog person. Or a cat person. She didn't have time for a pet, but she always paid attention to them when she visited friends who had them. Clean and brushed, Ghost Dog was gorgeous. As much as she wanted to spend the morning with him, the Fall Festival was starting at nine with or without her, and if she didn't show up on time, Faith would hand out all of the Halloween candy by 9:05.

Her shower was quick, but the water felt wonderful against

her tired body. Her eyes still burned from lack of sleep, but the blood flowing through her veins burned her in a different way. She would see Sarah this morning. And meet her daughter. As much as she wanted to dress up and look nice, she was required to wear her uniform.

"You're going to have to stay here, big guy. I just don't trust the town yet." His brown eyes were so trusting. He wagged his tail and stood by the door. "No, baby. I'll be back later to let you out, and we'll have a lunch date together, okay?" She adjusted her belt, grabbed her coat, slipped on her aviators, and patted the golden on his head before she slipped out of the front door. After checking her watch, she picked up the pace and headed to the station.

"Sheriff? You coming in?"

Faith's cheerful voice made Natalie smile. She clicked the button on her shoulder radio. "I'm thirty seconds out. What's going on?"

"You have a visitor."

Natalie's heart jumped. She cleared her throat. "I'll be there soon." It was kind of early for Sarah to be there, but like she said last night, six-year-old kids didn't sleep late. She entered the parking lot from the west side, since Main Street was blocked.

"The trailer looks fantastic, Faith." Natalie walked in the front door, wanting to see the wagon before the street was flooded with townspeople. Several businesses were putting up last-minute decorations or cooking the first round of early morning samples.

"Thanks, Boss. Mom and I hung around last night to finish up. Speaking of moms, yours is waiting for you in your office. I'm off to get more coffee brewed."

Even though she was always happy to see her mother, the corners of her mouth turned down when she realized it wasn't Sarah. "Hi, Mom. Why didn't you call me? I would have helped you unload your car."

Linda kissed her and waved her off. "Deputy David helped me."

Natalie peeked into the large canvas bags. "Did you overdo it again? What did you make?"

"Pumpkin rolls, pumpkin bread, ginger snaps, chocolate-chip bars, apple tarts, and a few other things."

"Mom. That's too much."

"If it helps the town accept you even more, then I'll do what I can."

Natalie sat in her chair and pointed for her mother to sit down. "I have news." Realizing that her statement sounded ominous, she quickly added, "It's good news."

Linda removed her hand from her heart and relaxed in her chair. "Don't scare me, Nat. What's the news?"

Natalie leaned forward and whispered, "I wanted to thank you and Judy for the date with Sarah last night. It went well."

"Whatever do you mean, thank me?" She winked at Natalie.

"Tanner's was too loud, so we went back to my place." She raised her palm up. "Now before you go thinking the worst or best thing, just know we had a chaperone."

"Well, was it a date date, or did you wimp out again?"

"She kissed me. She made the first move. But to be fair, I just didn't want to let her go when she wanted to leave."

"Tell me she's not handcuffed inside your house."

"Not yet." She gave her mom an exaggerated wink and smiled at her so hard that Linda questioned her again.

"Natalie Renee, you better start talking."

"I'm kidding. I let her go. Reluctantly. On both of our parts. It was a really nice date."

"That's great news, honey. I just hope she doesn't disappear again."

Natalie grabbed a cookie before Linda had a chance to smack her hand away. "Hey, this is my breakfast. I slept about four hours, and then I had to give Ghost Dog a bath because sleeping by the fireplace isn't his thing. He'd much rather sleep right next to me, and I'm not having a dirty dog in bed."

Linda reached out and cupped Natalie's chin. "You do look tired."

Natalie brushed her mom's hand away. "Thanks, Mom." She smacked her cheeks with the tips of her fingers to get more color into them.

"Sheriff? Should we open up?" Faith shouted.

"Why doesn't she use the intercom thingy?" Linda whispered.

"I can't even begin to explain her." Natalie grabbed a few bags of treats and met Faith by the front door. "Okay. What's the plan?"

"Let's get out there and show the town we're cool. At least the kids."

Natalie scowled at the cool morning. The sun was out, but still low, and it would be a few hours before their side of the street would feel its warmth. She set out paper cups while Linda brought out the Bunn carafe. David ran an extension cord from the front office out to the trailer. She wasted no time pouring herself a cup of coffee to warm her. She actually wanted to go home, slip into bed, and sleep for another four hours. She smiled when she remembered waking up to Ghost Dog next to her.

"People are starting to trickle in," Linda said.

"It'll take time for people to get past the Bradfords' trailer. This year they have baby lambs and probably tons of yummy stuff to eat." She looked at her mom. "But nothing nearly as good as ours. And who wants goat cheese this early in the morning when we have pastries and delicious baked goods?"

"Nice save, kiddo. Okay. I'm going to go walk around. You stay here and be charming, like always."

"Send people our way. Tell them we have cake and breads." It wasn't a competition really, but the winner always had bragging rights. And very few people wanted to hang out with local law enforcement, so all visitors were overly welcomed. Normally, Natalie would settle in and wait the day out shaking hands and smiling at people she pissed off or made happy at some point during the year. She spent most of the time talking to the elderly, who either wanted to complain about neighbors or tell them what the town used to be like when it had only about five hundred residents. To them, Spruce Mountain was a hopping town. They were always the first to oppose any upgrades or resist change of any kind.

"Sheriff, you have a visitor. Or two."

Natalie was in the closet gathering chairs to place in front of the trailer for people who wanted to sit and talk. "I'll be right there." Why did it always start so early? She carried four chairs out and almost dropped them when she saw her guests. Her heart turned into mush at seeing Sarah and her miniature, Harley, standing at the trailer looking over the selection of baked goods. Since her hands were full, she couldn't do a quick primp.

"Hi there." Sarah's smile made her knees weak.

"Good morning." Natalie placed the chairs against the trailer, adjusted her hat, and knelt. "You must be Harley." She offered her hand and melted a little more when Harley shook it.

"Hi, Sheriff."

Natalie tipped her hat at Harley and stood to face Sarah.

"Good morning to you." Sarah looked refreshed and beautiful. It was hard not to reach out and pull her close, but they were in public, and she was meeting Harley for the first time. "Harley is adorable."

"She couldn't wait to get down here. I thought we'd stop here first because I got an inside tip about baby lambs, and I have a feeling it's going to take a while before we circle back around, but I wanted to say good morning to you. How did you sleep?"

Natalie couldn't take her eyes off Sarah. She removed her hat and smoothed down her hair. "Well, I slept about four hours and woke up to a smelly dog right next to me."

"Sounds somewhat perfect," Sarah said.

"Not as good as it could have been." Natalie winked and turned to Harley. "Would you like some hot cocoa?"

Harley looked at Sarah. "Can I have some, Mom?"

"Might as well. I'm pretty sure this whole weekend is going to be a sugar rush with the festival today and Halloween tomorrow," Sarah said.

"Oh, what are you going to be for Halloween?" Natalie couldn't believe how much Harley and Sarah looked alike. Same brown eyes, same hair, same crooked smile, same single dimple that showed up only on the left cheek.

"I'm going to be Captain Marvel."

Natalie widened her eyes dramatically. "I love Captain Marvel. She's my hero. That's part of the reason why I'm sheriff."

"Do you know her?" Harley's innocent question made Natalie laugh.

"No, but I used to read comic books, and she was always my favorite character."

"You are a comic buff?" Sarah tilted her head.

"Ever since I could read. My collection is astounding."

Two things had saved Natalie from being a total outcast in school. Sports and comics. The jocks left her alone because she helped the school win championships, and the alternative kids who dressed in black and lived on sarcasm and nicotine appreciated her dedication to something cool. Sarah had probably forgotten that she collected comics. Natalie wasn't on Sarah's radar as much as Sarah was on hers. That was then, but this was now.

"Maybe you could show me your collection some time," Sarah said.

"How about tonight? After the festival winds down?" Natalie tried to act nonchalant and hoped Sarah couldn't tell how fast her heart was beating or see the sweat that always gathered at the back of her neck. She rested her hip against the trailer, trying to look cooler than she felt.

"I'd like that."

"Me, too." Harley smiled and looked at them.

Sarah was quick to answer while Natalie stammered and stuttered. "No, baby. Adults only. Besides, you and Aunt Judy are making apples tonight for trick-or-treat." She turned to Natalie and fake-swiped her brow. "How caramel apples can be handed out in today's world blows my mind."

She didn't say yes. Natalie arched her brow and waited for an answer. She got a quick nod. "Welcome to small-town America. Plus, they will be at the Veterans' Lodge, so not really randomly handed out."

"Good point. But there's still good old-fashioned knocking on doors and asking for candy, right? That hasn't changed, I hope."

"We still have that. Tomorrow will be a busy night, but not out of control, I hope," Natalie said. Halloween was normally quiet, with only a few harmless pranks. She patrolled the neighborhoods to crack down on any shenanigans. A part of her liked watching teenagers stress when she stopped them. "What's in the bag? Where are you all going? Don't you think you should be home? It's getting late out." Her favorite was always, "Don't let me find you still out on the streets when I circle back around."

"Well then, let's hope tonight is calmer for you."

"Or not." Where she got that kind of boldness from, she didn't know, but she was going with it because she could see the effect it had on Sarah. She liked how Sarah fiddled with the strap on her purse and had a hard time making eye contact.

"Or not."

Natalie cleared her throat. "Eight?"

"See you then."

"Sheriff?"

Natalie turned to Faith after she was done watching Sarah leave. "Yes?"

"Your smile is blinding. You might want to save some of that for the rest of the town, or else it's going to be a long day for you."

❖

"Hey there, buddy. Did you miss me? Huh? Did you miss me?"

Natalie greeted him with all the warmth that the golden greeted her with. She clipped on his leash and let him outside to do his business. The sun took the bite out of the low temperature, but it was obvious that winter wasn't too far away. She fixed him lunch and brushed his fur again now that it was completely dry. "Because you smell good now, I won't be upset if you accidentally crawl into my bed and snuggle with me. But maybe not tonight, okay?" Not that she was banking on having sex with Sarah tonight, but there was a high probability of some heavy making out. "Look. I have a date later, and I might need the space."

With the golden clean and gorgeous, Natalie snapped a few pictures of him to put on the website and send out to nearby counties. Now that she had him, it was time to buckle down and find his home.

"Okay. I have to get back to the festival. You be a very good boy, and I'll bring you home a cookie from Nana." Natalie gave him one last pat on his head and locked the door on her way out. She wasn't taking any chances. That dog was as slippery as an eel. She still had no idea how he'd got into her shed.

"What have I missed?" Natalie asked. She walked up to the trailer and did a quick inventory of what was left of the food and candy. "I was gone less than twenty minutes. How is everything almost gone?"

Faith looked away and rearranged the leftover mismatched napkins. "Everyone got hungry because it's lunchtime."

Natalie sighed. "Why don't you go walk around and grab some lunch? I've got the trailer."

"I can't wait to see the lambs. Ever since you told me, I've been itching to get my hands on them." Faith zipped up her coat and left Natalie alone with a half a bag of candy and nothing but crumbs from her mother's treats.

"I think we're about done."

Natalie stood when Sarah and Harley returned. "Did you see the lambs?"

"Oh, my gosh. They were so cute, and I got to feed them with a bottle." Harley's smile lit up her face, and the little dimple popped out.

Natalie took off her hat and, without even thinking, put it on Harley's tiny head. She giggled when it swallowed half her face. "It's a little big for you."

"Do you have a car with sirens and lights?"

"I do. It's parked out back."

"Can I see it? You should bring it here so that all the kids can climb in it and turn on the lights."

Natalie stood there stunned. This six-year-old child had a brilliant idea. Why hadn't they thought about that before? "You know what? That's a great idea. If you and your mom stand guard over the trailer, I'll go get the car right now."

"Go ahead. We've got this," Sarah said.

Natalie grabbed her keys and cut through the office to get to the parking lot. All these years she could have had bragging rights. Who didn't love to flip the lights on or talk on the radio? She asked the ladies at Creative Crafts to move the barricade so she could get the squad car next to the trailer. She opened the door and crooked her finger at Harley. "Great idea. Want to have a seat and play with the equipment?" Natalie locked up the guns every night, so nothing was in the car that Harley or any other kid could get hurt with. She switched on the radio and turned it to channel two. She showed Harley how to grab the speaker, press the button, and call her. "I'm going to walk across the street. You just hold down the button and talk."

Harley nodded seriously. She waited until Natalie crossed the street before lifting the handset. "Sheriff. Hi. I can see you."

Natalie spoke slowly into the walkie. "What are your coordinates, Deputy?"

"What?" That question was followed by giggles.

"What was your favorite thing in the festival?" Natalie asked.

"The lambs!" Harley forgot to hit the button, but Natalie could hear her joyful shout.

"Don't tell anyone, but it's my favorite thing, too." Natalie returned to the car when other kids showed interest and started gathering around. She crawled in on the passenger side and showed them how to turn on the lights and flip on the sirens, but did only one tiny burst because she didn't want to scare the animals. They all took turns talking on the loudspeaker until their parents pulled them away. "Harley, that was a great idea. Thank you."

"Thank you for humoring her," Sarah said. Her appreciative smile melted Natalie more. If she wasn't careful, by the end of the day, she would be a puddle of emotional goo.

"Can you take me for a ride?" Harley asked.

"No, baby. Sheriff Natalie is working. Maybe some other time."

Natalie squatted. "How about I pick you up for school on Monday morning, and we'll turn on the flashing lights and get you there in style?"

Harley's eyes widened. "That would be awesome."

"I mean if it's okay with your mom." Natalie thought she might have overstepped her boundaries, but Sarah's face lit up almost as much as Harley's.

"That's okay with me. That just means you have to be up and ready early."

"I will. I promise." Harley crossed her heart with sincerity.

"Let's go. Say good-bye. It's time for a nap for both of us." Sarah took Harley's hand and gently pulled her away from Natalie.

"Text me later and let me know if you can get away?" Natalie tried hard to keep the desperation out of her voice.

"Check your phone, Sheriff."

Natalie pulled it out and smiled.

CHAPTER TEN

S arah was spending too much time getting ready. Natalie texted that she would pick her up at eight because they had eight-fifteen dinner reservations. Even though it was chilly, she decided on a wool skirt, black sweater, and black knee boots. The outfit was probably too chic for Spruce Mountain, but she missed dressing up and looking good. When was the last time she was on a date?

"Mom, you look so pretty."

Harley stood in the doorway. Sarah noticed her Disney-themed nightgown was getting a bit too small. She reached down and picked her up. "Thank you, baby. You know you're getting too big for me to pick you up, and that makes me sad."

"Why does that make you sad?"

"Because that means my baby is growing up." Sarah kissed her cheek and put her down. "Aren't you supposed to be helping Aunt Judy?" She knew Harley was going to have a hard time going to sleep tonight with all the sugar she'd consumed at the festival and making the caramel apples tonight.

"She told me to tell you the sheriff is here."

"Natalie's here?" Sarah looked at herself one last time in the mirror. She'd straightened her hair and pulled it back in a single clip, creating a classic yet sophisticated look. "I'd better go. Lead the way." Sarah followed Harley up the stairs and grabbed the railing when she saw Natalie talking with Aunt Judy in the foyer. She was so beautiful, so commanding, so tall. Her blond hair was curled and hung loosely around her shoulders. She was wearing all black, including ankle boots that added to her height. Sarah licked her lips, remembering the last time they were alone and the powerful kiss they'd shared. "Hi." When Natalie looked up at her, she saw raw hunger in her eyes that was quickly covered when Aunt Judy cleared her throat.

"You two better get going. Saturday night in Spruce is hopping. Come on, Harley. You are needed in the kitchen. We have to wrap the apples before bed," Judy said. She put her hands on Harley's tiny shoulders and marched her into the kitchen. "Have a nice time, ladies. I won't wait up."

Sarah chuckled nervously and made herself look at Natalie. "You look really nice. I've always loved the color of your hair."

Natalie smiled and blushed at the compliment. "Thank you. I always hated it growing up. People teased me."

"They were stupid. Every single one of them," Sarah said. She opened the door and followed Natalie out to her Jeep, pausing when Natalie opened the door for her.

"What's the matter?"

Sarah turned to Natalie, who was so close she felt her body heat. She wanted to wrap her arms around Natalie's waist and walk into her warmth. She smelled like lavender and firewood. She must have started a fire when she got home after the festival. The scent was faint, but it made Sarah smile. She loved that smell. "I can't climb into your Jeep."

"What do you mean?"

"My skirt is…restrictive." Sarah was embarrassed because she'd purposely worn a skirt that hugged her hips and her thighs so Natalie would notice. But the skirt landed past her knees, so stepping up into the Jeep wasn't an option. She hadn't thought things through when she decided to go for the sexy look.

"Shit. I'm sorry. I wasn't thinking."

"Let's take my car. It's a boring sedan, but at least I can get in it. Will you drive though? I don't know where we're going," Sarah said.

"Remind me to buy a new car tomorrow. A four-door."

Sarah smiled at Natalie when she handed her the car fob. "Or I could just never wear this skirt again."

"That's a negative. I want you to wear that skirt every day, even when it's summer."

"Wool in summer would be torture."

"Okay. I'll make an exception."

Sarah turned her head and squelched the need to shiver from the look that Natalie gave her. It was the kind of look she read about in romance novels and saw in movies, but never in real life. If she were bolder and more experienced, she would speak up and tell Natalie to skip dinner and take her straight to her house so they could pick up where they'd left off last night.

"And just like that, we're here." Natalie put the car in park and pointed to the quaint little restaurant sandwiched between an antique shop and a shoe-repair store.

"I've driven by several times and never even saw it before now," Sarah said. She opened the car door and waited for Natalie to climb out from behind the wheel.

"I haven't been here in a while, but it's a town favorite. The seafood is always a safe bet, but you can't screw up a steak either," Natalie said.

The host sat them by a wide window. Their view was the full moon shining down on the mountain. Sarah leaned forward, wineglass in hand, and offered a toast. "Here's to a new beginning in an old place."

Natalie lifted her glass and clinked it gently against Sarah's. "Here's to coming home again."

❖

Natalie stood in front of the door when she unlocked it. "Just in case Ghost Dog tries to escape."

Sarah watched how happy Natalie looked as she greeted the sweet dog. He was so gentle with her, but she saw that he was still somewhat skittish. "Well, it looks like he's found a nice home here. Have you thought about keeping him?" She let him smell her hand before she petted the top of his head.

"I don't want to keep what isn't mine. After I've exhausted all possibilities, I'll consider it or give him to my mother. She could use another friend. But right now, I'm going to take him out. I won't be long." Natalie promisingly squeezed Sarah's hand before she leashed him and slipped out the door.

Sarah walked into the living room and looked at the framed photos on the mantel. She smiled at the picture of Natalie and her parents. They were always at the high school games supporting her. Sarah was too busy trying to fit in with the kids to get to know anybody's parents, but she was always aware of Natalie's because she was focused on Natalie, too. The other photos were of people she assumed were family. Same blond hair, same smile. Cousins, aunts, and uncles probably. The one baby picture on the mantel was unmistakably Natalie. Adorable hair, beautiful dark-blue eyes, and the precious smile that captivated her even in the photo. Sarah turned when she heard Natalie and Ghost Dog return. She waved the frame at Natalie. "What a beautiful baby you were. And wearing a dress."

"I don't have too many occasions to wear one here in Spruce, so my wardrobe is limited. I think the last time I wore a dress was for my cousin's wedding."

"Oh, I want to see a photo of that," Sarah said.

Sarah didn't move when Natalie gently took the photo from her hands and put it back on the mantel. She forgot to breathe when Natalie stepped closer and touched her cheek. She slightly shook when Natalie kissed her softly. "I don't know what's better. A heated kiss from you or the soft, gentle ones. Both leave me breathless."

Natalie undid the clip that held Sarah's hair back. "You always talk about my hair, but we never talk about yours. It looks great long. And I love the highlights."

Sarah closed her eyes. When was the last time she felt beautiful? When was the last time somebody made her feel beautiful? "Thank you." Natalie's lips brushed hers again, softly, sweetly.

"I'm going to start a fire. Then I'm going to make us a drink. Get comfortable."

Sarah sat in the middle of the couch, giving Natalie very little doubt about her intent. She fluffed up her hair while Natalie's back was turned and tried to make herself look as sexy as she felt.

"What do you want to drink?"

"I'd love a glass of water, please."

"Coming right up."

Sarah barely waited for Natalie to sit down before she reached for her. Natalie didn't hesitate. They kissed, and just like before, their chemistry ignited immediately. Sarah didn't remember how she got on her back. She didn't care. Having Natalie on top of her was a dream come true. She slipped her hands up Natalie's sweater and sighed at how soft her skin was. Hearing Natalie moan fueled the fire inside her. She moved her hands higher and tried to spread her legs to accommodate Natalie's hips, but her skirt was too tight. She growled in frustration.

Natalie broke the kiss. "Are you okay?"

"I'm so mad that I wore this skirt. I was going for sexy, but I can't move at all. Bad decision."

"Are you kidding me? I couldn't breathe when you walked down those stairs. You look amazing and feel incredible. I have an idea." Natalie sat up and pulled Sarah to her. "Follow me."

"Where are we going?" Sarah looked deep into Natalie's eyes and smiled when she realized Natalie was slowly falling backward on the couch. When they finally settled, Sarah was resting comfortably between Natalie's legs. She arched her brow. "Oh. I like this." She leaned up and pulled her skirt up past her knees. She had more freedom as she sank back into Natalie. "Oh. I like this a lot."

Natalie pulled Sarah down to her mouth. "So, this is okay?"

She liked the way Natalie asked and looked her in the eye, as though she was the most important thing. She kissed Natalie softly. "This is very okay." In the span of about three seconds, Natalie had spread her legs wider and had both hands on Sarah's back, holding her close. Sarah closed her eyes at the intimacy of their cores pressed together and their bodies flush. They kissed softly, but the second Sarah felt Natalie's hands under her sweater, the kiss deepened. She almost smiled at how Natalie's fingers stopped and fluttered when she realized Sarah wasn't wearing a bra. She wasn't wearing panties either and wondered if Natalie would discover that, too.

When she felt Natalie's fingers brush along her ribs, moving closer to her breast, Sarah arched her back to give her full access. She broke the kiss and watched Natalie's face as she guided Natalie's hand to her breast. Natalie's eyes narrowed when her fingers cupped it, but she never broke eye contact. Sarah was the one who closed her eyes first. She couldn't process everything—the physical closeness, the overpowering emotions that flooded her head and her heart. Natalie was intense and knew exactly what Sarah wanted. She opened her eyes when Natalie pushed up her sweater and watched as Natalie slowly sucked her erect nipple. She moaned when she felt Natalie's tongue stroke her sensitive skin and shook with desire at how Natalie knew exactly what she needed. Sarah pulled away and took off her sweater.

Natalie fell back onto the pillows and stared up at her. "I can't believe how beautiful you are. I can't believe you're here, in my house, in my arms."

Sarah didn't feel embarrassed to be half-naked on top of the woman she wanted to be intimate with. Natalie touched her hair and gently pulled Sarah down to her mouth. Every kiss got better, but how was that possible when the one before was so perfect? "I can't believe I'm here either." Sarah placed her hand on Natalie's chest. She was afraid to want someone this much. She'd spent the last year of her life picking up the pieces and not focusing on just herself. Now, in this moment, it was all about her and Natalie.

She kissed Natalie's neck and collarbone. She slid down her and smiled when her hip pressed against Natalie's pussy and she moaned. Very slowly, she pushed up Natalie's sweater and placed tiny kisses on her stomach. She kissed Natalie's hands when they slipped down to pull the sweater over her head. Sarah leaned up to give her room and sighed with pleasure when she saw Natalie's full breasts in a sexy black bra. She traced her fingers along the lacy edge, dipping inside until she held the beautifully hardened nipple in the palm of her hand. Natalie was up on her elbows watching her, her eyes hooded with passion. She licked her lips as her breath quickened.

"I have been wanting to touch you forever," Sarah said.

"You can't possibly know the restraint I'm showing right now."

Sarah swallowed hard at how sexy and raw Natalie's voice was. She ran her fingers down Natalie's hard stomach and pressed her palm flat on her abs. "You can't possibly know how fucking sexy you look right now." She placed a kiss on the swell of Natalie's breast. She slipped the strap down her shoulder to loosen the lace and pulled it back to take Natalie's nipple into her mouth. Natalie's hiss of pleasure was music to Sarah's ears. Her hand on the back of Sarah's neck encouraged her to continue kissing and sucking. Sarah needed more but didn't want to push things. Her first time with Natalie shouldn't be on a couch and what was technically their second date. When was the last time she had an orgasm? It was before she returned to Spruce. She took a deep breath and pulled back. "I'm sorry. I'm so sorry. I'm jumping in too soon."

Natalie pulled her down and kissed her. "It's okay. Just being here with you, holding you, is a dream come true."

Sarah rested her head on Natalie's shoulder and listened to her rapid heartbeat. She couldn't deny that Natalie felt something for her. She could tell by the way Natalie looked at her and the words she whispered that they had a strong bond. But was she being honest with Natalie? Spruce Mountain was a place to regroup, not a place to set roots. It was never in the plan to stay. Maybe a year or two, but forever? That scared her. Was this the best place to raise her daughter? Would Harley have the best education or childhood living in a small town? Why the fuck was she thinking about this now? She sighed. Because she wanted to be fair to Natalie. She didn't want to do the same thing again.

"Are you okay?" Natalie stroked the back of Sarah's head.

"I am. I'm sorry. I didn't mean for this to get out of control.

I don't want you to think less of me because I threw myself at you and then pulled back. I just want to do this right and not ruin something by rushing, you know?"

She felt Natalie's lips press against the top of her head. "There's no rush. I've waited seventeen years, and I can wait a little longer."

Sarah put her hand on Natalie's heart and kept it there. She felt Natalie pull a blanket off the back of the couch and cover them up. With Natalie's arms around her and the warmth of their bodies pressed together, she fell asleep feeling loved for the first time in a long time.

CHAPTER ELEVEN

Halloween was a day of highs and lows. Natalie always worked to keep the peace and to make sure the pranks were minimal. She loved seeing the kids dress up in costumes and parade through the quaint neighborhoods, but she hated chasing kids who threw rocks at houses and cars.

It had rained earlier in the day, a cold, uncomfortable rain that hinted of snow in their future, but that wasn't what put Natalie in a foul mood. She woke up alone and on the couch. Sarah had left sometime during the night, and she slept through it. She left a sweet note, but Natalie was sad that she didn't say good-bye. She wanted a tight hug and a kiss. Instead she got a lukewarm shower that didn't help improve her mood. There was a text message from Sarah this morning asking her to text when she woke up so she could pick her up and get the Jeep. She even took out her foul mood on Ghost Dog when she took him outside.

"It's too cold, buddy. Can we speed things up a little bit?" He must've picked up on her vibe because he went straight to his bed when they walked in the house and avoided her eyes.

She brewed a cup of coffee and grabbed a banana and sat on the couch staring at Ghost Dog. "Come here, boy." She reached out her hand as a peace offering. He slowly walked over to her and sniffed it. She stroked his soft ears and patted the couch. He jumped on it and rested his head in her lap. "I'm sorry. I didn't mean to snap at you. I should be in a good mood, right? Sarah and I had a pretty good night. Nothing about it was bad. So, why don't I feel great?"

Ghost Dog thumped his tail softly and perked up when she opened the banana.

"Do you like bananas? Can dogs even eat bananas?" She broke off a small bite and gave it to him. He wolfed it down and stared at her. "What? You want another bite?" He rolled onto his back and looked up at her, his tongue lolling out of the side of his mouth. Then he gave a small woof, followed by a begging motion of his front paws in the air. "Well, I'll be damned. I've found your weakness." She quickly googled to see if bananas were good for dogs. She gave him another bite. "Moderation, it says, so this can be your treat." Just having him in her lap so happy about a banana improved her mood.

She shot off a text to Sarah and told her she was available anytime. As much as she thought about having Betty drop her off, she wanted to see Sarah and ensure that everything was okay with them. Things had gotten hot and heavy fast, but then fizzled. It was as if a switch inside Sarah had flipped on, and Natalie wanted to know why.

I can be there in ten minutes.

Natalie had no makeup on and was in yoga pants and a sweatshirt. She jumped up from the couch, causing Ghost Dog to twist and almost fall off. "Sorry, buddy. I've got to get ready. Sarah's on her way over." She was running a brush through her damp hair when the doorbell rang. Ghost Dog gave a deep bark but was wagging his tail. He knew it was Sarah.

"Hi. Hang on. Let me get some shoes on. Come on in," Natalie said.

Sarah grabbed her hand before she got far. "Hang on, Nat." She pulled Natalie close. "Two things."

"What's going on?" Natalie put her hands on Sarah's hips and waited. She was so beautiful that Natalie could stand in the foyer and stare at her all day if Sarah would let her.

"I need to apologize for last night."

"Not at all. Well, maybe the part about you leaving and not telling me."

"Actually, I told you, and you grumbled something about being cold, so I covered you up, and you drifted off to sleep. But that's not what I meant. I'm sorry for leading you on and then stopping. Look, can we sit down?"

"Of course. Let's go sit on the couch."

Natalie sat on one side and allowed Sarah the opportunity to sit wherever she wanted. Sarah sat directly beside her, their thighs touching.

"I really like you, Natalie. I always have. I screwed up before, but I want to take things slow this time and do it right. I pushed too hard last night."

"Hey, hey. I wanted you last night, without a doubt, but we can go at whatever pace you want. I meant what I said. I will wait for you."

Sarah nodded and looked down. "You've been so wonderful to me, to my family. Thank you for understanding."

Natalie squeezed her hand. "What was the second thing?"

"This." Sarah smiled before she kissed Natalie.

Fire spread through Natalie, and she wondered if she was going to last. She pulled Sarah onto her lap and deepened the kiss. She couldn't help it. She wanted to touch Sarah but didn't know what was acceptable. "Is this okay?"

"Definitely."

Sarah was breathing harder than she was before the kiss.

Natalie knew she felt something, too. More than passion. She ran her finger over Sarah's cheek and across her bottom lip. "I'm sorry I was grumpy with you last night when you tried to wake me. Apparently, I'm not used to people staying over."

"That's a good thing to hear. I'm fine with you sharing your bed with Ghost Dog only. And his bath was a good call."

"Fresh sheets, fresh dog," Natalie said. She patted Sarah's hip. "Come on. Let's go get the Jeep. I have a few errands to run and need to make sure Mom has everything she needs for tonight. Halloween is a big event around here."

Sarah stood and pulled Natalie up with her. "Harley is beyond excited. She's going to wear herself out before things even get started. What time do most people start?"

"About six. I'll begin patrolling about five."

"What? You aren't going to pass out candy?" Sarah tickled her softly.

Natalie grasped her hands and entwined their fingers before she kissed her. What had happened felt sweet and made her feel like they were a couple. It was hard not to read too much into the moment. "I'll have a big bag with me in the car. Plus, nobody comes over to the house. I'm at the end of the road, and the house backs up to the woods." Natalie slipped into her jacket and grabbed the keys. "This way, I can see all the costumes and talk to the kids."

Sarah kissed her swiftly. "You're adorable. Just a softie."

Natalie shrugged. "What can I say? I get to be the big, bad-ass sheriff three hundred and sixty-two days out of the year. I need a few days to be me."

"So, Halloween, Christmas, and what else?" Sarah held up her fingers, counting down the holidays.

"Thanksgiving is my favorite."

"Why?"

Natalie could feel the heat flood her cheeks. It was a

holiday that was overlooked, and she was embarrassed to say why she liked it so much. "I just have so much in this life to be thankful for." She shrugged like it was no big deal.

Sarah stopped her. "You're right. Thanksgiving is special and should be celebrated. I have a lot to be thankful for, too. Come on. Let's go before Harley blows up my phone. We have to complete a few alterations on her costume before tonight."

Natalie turned to Ghost Dog. "You be a good boy, and I'll be home soon."

"I really think you should keep him," Sarah said.

"He's perfect, but he might be somebody's dog, and if I get attached and have to give him up, I'll never recover. I don't think he wants to break my heart."

Ghost Dog wagged his tail and gave her a gentle, low woof, as if he understood her. Natalie blew him a kiss as she shut the door. She was quiet during the short drive, but didn't hesitate when Sarah reached out to hold her hand.

"Do you want to come in for a minute? I'm sure Harley is dying to show the town sheriff, who loves Captain Marvel, her costume."

Natalie thought about everything she needed to do today, but no way was she going to tell Sarah no. "Only for a few minutes."

"Sheriff Natalie. You're here. Look at my costume." Harley stood with her tiny fists on her hips.

It took all of Natalie's energy not to pick her up and squeeze her because she was so damn adorable. Instead, she mimicked Harley and put her hands on her own hips. "You look awesome like that."

"Now go take it off before you spill your lunch on it. We'll alter it closer to when we leave."

Eye roll followed by an exaggerated huff. "What time are we going?"

"If you want to know where all the good places are, I'd suggest hitting the lodge first. That gets started about five. Most of the trick-or-treaters begin around six in the neighborhood."

Sarah arched her brow in disbelief.

"What? I thought you wanted the schedule?"

Harley danced around the living room. "That's in only five hours. Woohoo!" She threw her hands up and pretended to fly around the kitchen, making whooshing sounds as she weaved around everyone.

"Hi, Natalie. It's good to see you again," Judy said.

"Are you feeling better?" Natalie winked at her, remembering Judy's feigned headache two days earlier.

"I feel wonderful. How about you?"

Natalie happily nodded. "Okay, ladies. I have to check on my mom. I will see you out and about this evening. Be safe. Bring extra flashlights and dress in layers." She slipped into the cold Jeep and waited for it to warm up before driving the ten blocks to her mother's house. It always made her sad when she pulled up in the driveway because her dad had always met her at the door, and now he was gone. He would have been proud of her and how far she'd come.

She rested her head on the steering wheel and wallowed in memories for a few moments before walking up to the door. She missed him so much. Their family seemed so small without him. He had been a bear of a man, who stood six inches taller than Natalie and sported the bushiest red beard. She joked that he looked like a serial killer when he wore flannel and a beanie, but he assured her it was proper lumberjack attire and accessorized with a red ax that he called Brenda. He always threatened he would greet her dates dressed like that, but she never brought anybody home. He never got the chance to meet anybody she dated. She wondered if he knew about her crush on Sarah or if he even knew who she was.

"Hi, sweetie. How are you this morning?" Linda kissed her on the cheek and poured her a cup of coffee.

"I'm tired, but good. How was your night?"

"I wrote for a bit, then watched television. Nothing exciting, but I understand you had an exciting night." Linda smiled at her knowingly.

Natalie threw up her hands. "Is there no such thing as discretion anymore?"

"I was just guessing, but it seems I was right."

Natalie playfully growled at her mother. "You know, it was a good night, and we set some boundaries." She continued at her mother's encouraging nod. "So, we were in the moment, and Sarah pulled away because she decided it was a bad idea to rush into everything. She wants to take us slow." She air-quoted the word us for effect.

Linda squeezed her hand. "That's a good thing. She's coming off a divorce and has a child. That's a sensitive spot to be in."

"Harley's already met me, and it's not like I'm out playing the field." Natalie took a deep breath and confessed, "I've wanted Sarah for a long time."

"Honey, everyone knows that. It's not a surprise. I think you've come together at the perfect time in both of your lives. Sometimes love takes longer to find people, and sometimes it leaves people too soon."

"I know, Mom. I was just thinking about Dad when I pulled up. I miss him."

"I miss him, too. But I have you and friends and a lot to still be thankful for in this life."

Natalie didn't think her mother would ever date again but was hopeful. She didn't want her mother to be alone forever, but she also understood what it meant to yearn for someone.

"Okay, enough of the sad and sappy. Let's get you ready

for Halloween. I see you've decorated the porch already."
Linda was known for her big holiday displays, but the last few
years, she'd toned it down. Guilt rested on Natalie's shoulders
as she realized she should have helped her mom get set up, but
she was too wrapped up in her own world.

"I think I have enough candy, and I still have the lanterns
to line the steps for the children."

"Do we need to do anything?"

Linda shook her head. "Nope. How about we eat some
lunch and relax before the chaos hits?"

"Perfect. I doubt I'll get dinner, so let's fatten me up."
Natalie patted her stomach, knowing full well her mother was
not only going to ensure she ate a proper lunch but would pack
a brown bag for when she patrolled later.

❖

"It sure is quiet out, Sheriff."

Joshua was patrolling the other side of the small town and
reported only a few pranks and stopped two boys with three
dozen eggs. The oval bombs were confiscated, and the kids
were taken home to embarrassed parents.

"I'm not seeing much either." It wasn't that she wanted
things to happen, but she was bored and, truthfully wanted to
spend the evening with Sarah and Harley. It was too soon to
be a fixture in their lives, but tonight was all about fun, and
Harley had childhood innocence and enjoyed Halloween so
much. She didn't even see them out trick-or-treating, though
she made several trips over to their neighborhood. "It's ten. I
think we can call it a night. Anything that happens this late is
a crime, and we'll deal with it in the morning."

She looked down at her phone, hoping for a text message
from Sarah, but the only thing she saw was a temperature of

forty-two and a time of 10:04. A photo of Ghost Dog was her wallpaper, and she smiled at his beautiful face. She'd go home to him and would see Sarah in the morning when she picked up Harley for school.

"Hello, sweet boy! Did we have any trick-or-treaters?" He seemed calm and wagged his tail, indicating everything was quiet on the home front. Even though it was chilly, Natalie walked him through the neighborhood. He had been locked up since five, and she felt guilty. Maybe one day, he could go to work with her or be around other people. He was comfortable with Sarah already, but she was worried about him with Harley. Since she didn't know his history, she didn't know his triggers. They returned, and after she took a long, hot shower, they crawled into bed as if they did it every night. Natalie remembered rubbing his ears before drifting off to sleep. When the alarm rang seven hours later, she woke in the same position, but Ghost Dog had crawled up closer and was resting his head next to hers.

❖

Natalie starched her uniform and ironed it carefully, as if she was under inspection. Her badge was polished and hat firmly pressed on her head. It was an important morning. She had a promise to keep. She wished she had a kid's deputy badge or a small campaign hat for Harley but came up empty-handed. She vowed to get more involved with the schools and have fun things to pass out. Interacting with kids was proving to be beneficial. Maybe getting through to them now would help them later during their struggling teenage years.

"Okay, big guy. I'm out. Be good, and I'll see you at lunch." She wiped off the back seat and picked up every tiny piece of paper, ensuring it was clean and ready for her next passenger. It took five minutes to get to Sarah's house. She parked on the street and marched up the stairs.

"Can I help you?"

Natalie wasn't prepared for a stranger to open the door. "Hi. I'm Natalie. I'm here to take Harley to school." It was hard to keep the confusion out of her voice. The stranger rubbed her hands over her face to wake up and smirked at Natalie.

"Sorry we didn't call you, Sheriff. I'm taking her to school today."

"Where's Sarah?"

"She's in the shower. I'm Francine, and it's nice to meet you." She leaned her shoulder up against the door frame and crossed her arms across her chest as if she belonged there. She was attractive, with short, dark hair, light-blue eyes, and a tan that didn't make sense this time of year. Her boxer briefs and tank top showed off a sinewy body and left little to the imagination.

Natalie stood face-to-face with the ex-wife. She tamped down the need to push past Francine and find out what was going on. Instead, she kept her cool. "I'm Natalie. Can you please tell Sarah and Harley that I stopped by and that I will catch up with them later?" There was a bit of a snark in her, and her tone might have implied she was more involved with them than she was. Francine was doing the same.

She narrowed her eyes. "Of course I will. You have a nice day." And without so much as a good-bye, Francine looked away and closed the door right in Natalie's face.

CHAPTER TWELVE

Sarah instantly exploded with anger when she opened the front door and saw Francine standing in the doorway with a duffel bag. "What could you possibly be doing here?" She did nothing to hide her dismay.

"Whoa. Relax. I have a conference in Portland that starts Tuesday and thought I would come up here and hang out with Harley for Halloween. I'm only here for a day," Francine said.

"And it never occurred to you to call me and see if it was okay to just stop in?"

"I don't need permission to see my daughter, Sarah." Francine held out her arms when Harley yelled out her name and raced over to her.

Sarah gritted her teeth and smiled at Harley. "Look who's here, baby."

"Francine. Guess who I'm going to be for Halloween?"

Rather than try to guess, Francine shrugged. "Tell me."

"Captain Marvel. Because she's cool and fights the bad aliens."

"Perfect. I can't wait to see your costume. Want me to take you trick-or-treating?"

Sarah almost laughed when Harley shrugged. "Mom's taking me, but I guess you can come with us."

"Hello, Francine." Judy's voice was clipped and unemotional.

"Aunt Judy. How are you?" Francine asked. She threw her duffel bag by the front door and kicked off her boots.

Sarah hated how comfortable Francine made herself. She was no longer a member of this family, yet she paraded like a peacock in front of them, as if she not only was still a loving part, but head of household.

"I'm well. We're all doing fine. Thanks for asking."

"Apparently Francine will be trick-or-treating with us tonight. She's attending a conference in Portland on Tuesday so thought it would be a nice gesture to swing by and disrupt our plans." Nope. She didn't intend to go down without a fight. Maybe Francine would not feel welcomed and leave early.

"Come on. Don't be like that. I haven't seen Harley in months."

Sarah turned and hissed. "Whose fault is that? I thought we discussed this already."

Francine didn't back down. "Let's talk in the morning." She turned to Harley. "Why don't you put on your costume so I can see this Captain Somebody costume."

"Can I put it on, Mom?"

"No. Francine can wait until five. It's only three now. After you eat you can put it on, okay?"

Harley wasn't a child who pouted or threw tantrums. She had Sarah's gentle disposition. "Okay. That's soon. Can I play on the iPad for a bit?"

Sarah nodded. Secretly she loved that Francine's visit had very little effect on Harley. She waited until Harley was out of the room. "You can't just stop by when you want. That's not how this works."

"She's my daughter."

"No, she's my daughter. Remember when you dragged

your feet on adopting her? You have zero rights with her. I'm allowing this visit strictly as a courtesy, but don't ever drop in unannounced again." She clenched her fists at her sides. She was just finding her footing here in Spruce Mountain, and the last thing she needed was her past blowing up her future.

"I helped raise her. Don't forget that." Francine puffed up her chest and stood taller.

"Oh, please. You were too busy playing doctor with everyone to give us a second thought." This was not a conversation she wanted to have in front of Aunt Judy or within earshot of Harley.

Francine held up her hands. "I get it. I'm not staying. I came up on a whim because the conference was so close. I'm not trying to win you back or upset anything you've done here. Truthfully. I come in peace."

Sarah backed down and nodded. "Okay. I can respect that. I just don't want to confuse Harley, and I need to keep my sanity, too."

Francine rested her hands on Sarah's shoulders. Sarah stiffened immediately and stepped out of the familiar embrace. It wasn't appropriate. Francine had crossed too many lines in the span of ten minutes.

"Are you hungry, Francine? Do you want anything to eat?" Judy yelled out from the kitchen.

"Always. I can't remember the last time I had a home-cooked meal."

"Well, tonight we are having fried chicken and macaroni and cheese. It was Harley's request. In the meantime, I have leftover pot roast and mashed potatoes I can heat up if you can't wait."

"That sounds delicious. I'd love a plate. Thanks, Judy."

Sarah remembered that Francine had the metabolism and energy level of a chipmunk. She ate a lot but ate healthily.

She was always snacking on nuts or fruit. At least Harley had gotten her good eating habits from Francine. Sarah stood there awkwardly, trying to figure out what to talk about or even if she wanted to be in the same room with her ex. It wasn't fair for Aunt Judy to have to entertain her uninvited guest, so she pulled out a dining room chair and sat down. It was going to be a long, stressful evening, one she dreaded even though she loved Halloween as much as Harley did.

❖

By five, Sarah needed space. Everything about Francine annoyed her. How she had stayed married to somebody so shallow and superficial amazed her. What had happened to her back then? Maybe being away from Francine and surrounding herself with good, honest people like Natalie, Linda, Aunt Judy, and Uncle Bob had changed her for the better. "It's time. Who's ready?"

"Yay!" Harley raced to put on her boots.

Sarah made Harley wear tights and a sweatshirt under her costume because the temperature was going to drop after the sun set. "You look great, kiddo."

"Hopefully, I'll see Sheriff Natalie out tonight."

"She's working, but I bet we run into her." Sarah was too nervous to even think of the possibility. What would she say? How would Natalie take it? She was sure Natalie would understand that Francine being with them wasn't her doing. New relationships were tricky though. Misunderstandings stressed her out. "Let's go." Aunt Judy sat in the front seat, while Harley and Francine sat in the back. Sarah drove slower than the speed limit to avoid any unnecessary spillage in the trunk. They had all worked so hard on the apples, and the last thing they needed was a sharp stop and the apples to tumble out of the pans.

By eight, everyone was exhausted, Harley's bag was filled with more candy than Sarah would ever allow her to eat, and the foursome had hit most of the neighborhoods Natalie suggested. Sarah was still getting used to the good areas of town. Not that there were any bad, but some of the houses were a bit run-down. She was surprised, and somewhat relieved, that they never crossed paths with Natalie. Sarah didn't send her a message, telling herself it was because Natalie was working and she shouldn't disturb her, but really it was because Sarah didn't want to explain Francine. Once they got home, she expected Francine to grab her things and leave. What she didn't expect was Aunt Judy to bring bedding and place it on the couch in front of Francine.

"Thanks, Aunt Judy," Francine said.

"What's going on here?" Sarah's voice was one octave higher, as the day's frustration mounted on her heart and conscience.

"It's late, and Francine asked if she could crash here and head out in the morning. I figured we'd all be asleep within the hour anyway."

Sarah heard the sharpness of Aunt Judy's voice and conceded. By the time she got Harley bathed and in bed, it would be close to nine. Everyone needed to decompress. She and Harley would stay downstairs until morning. "Okay. Say good night to everyone, baby." She wisely took Harley's candy and waited for her to say good night to Aunt Judy and Francine. Uncle Bob was still at the lodge and would be for hours. "Sleep well, Francine." Sarah nodded at her, kissed Aunt Judy's cheek, and led Harley to their private space in the basement.

Not once did Harley bring up Francine's name when she was getting tucked into bed. When Sarah carefully asked her what she thought about Francine being there, Harley shrugged and continued talking about all the things they saw, and who gave her the most candy, and what her favorite kind was. "So, you're not mad that she's here?"

"No. I don't like that she makes you mad."

Out of the mouths of babes, Sarah thought. "I'm sorry. She just surprised me because she didn't call and we weren't expecting her. I had different plans for us tonight."

"I still had a lot of fun."

Sarah pressed a kiss to Harley's forehead. "I did, too, baby. And that's the important thing. Get some sleep. You have school tomorrow."

❖

It had slipped Sarah's mind completely that Natalie was going to take Harley to school until she was filing away *Wynonna Earp* graphic novels and saw an illustration of a sheriff on one of the covers. She sent a text to Natalie for the first time in almost twenty-four hours.

How was your night? We looked for you but never crossed paths. She inserted a sad-face emoji.

She watched as bubbles popped up, then disappeared. Natalie must be busy. The day after Halloween had probably resulted in several trick calls that she and the deputies had to field.

Francine stayed later, insisting she wanted to take Harley to school, and they walked her in together. Sarah gritted her teeth the entire time and breathed the heaviest sigh of relief when she watched Francine head out of town. What a stressful twenty-four hours. She hoped Francine didn't pull this stunt on the way back to Texas. Sarah made it crystal clear that she didn't like the spontaneous pop-in and her aunt's hospitality wouldn't be extended a second time.

You were pretty busy last night.

Her heart sank at the passive-aggressive message. Somehow Natalie knew. Of course she knew. The town was small, and nothing spread faster than gossip. Everybody saw them together. Somebody was bound to tell Natalie.

Got a surprise visit from the ex. Wasn't expecting her, but Aunt Judy wouldn't let me throw her out.

She seemed pretty comfortable.

You saw us?

No. But I stopped by to pick Harley up for school this morning, and Francine informed me that she had it handled.

Sarah groaned in frustration.

I'm so sorry, Nat. It wasn't planned. She had no right to tell you that. The last several hours have been extremely stressful with her here, but she left this morning, and I made it very clear that she didn't have the right to barge into our lives anymore.

She didn't want to over-explain herself. What had happened wasn't something that would continue to occur, and as much as she wanted Natalie to know, she thought that if she pressed, she might seem guilty of something that didn't happen.

It's okay. It was a busy night, and this morning we've been running around answering calls. Did Harley have a good time?

They were maneuvering around the awkwardness, and Sarah said a little prayer of thanks that Natalie trusted her this early into their relationship.

She did. She looked for you. It was sweet.

Smiley face. *Okay. I have to go. I'll call you later.*

Please do.

And just like that, all was right in the world. Lunch was a quick bagel from the café as the afternoon flew by. Harley had asked if she could stay in aftercare to talk about Halloween with her two new best friends. Sarah agreed and told her she would pick her up at five. She would spend the afternoon researching how to start her own firm, since staying in Spruce Mountain was sounding like a pretty good idea. Harley was making friends at school, and even though Sarah had a job, it wasn't going to pay for her own place and all their living expenses.

Mary tapped her on her shoulder. "We're closing in five minutes."

Sarah looked at her in surprise. It was almost five? "Where did the day go?"

"Are you finding what you're looking for?"

"Definitely. It's overwhelming, but I made some progress. Thanks for your help." Sarah packed up her bag and walked the short distance to the school. The afternoon was cold, and she was thankful she'd made Harley take her heavier coat today, after much protest. She walked into the front office, and the only remaining receptionist looked up.

"Ms. Eastman. Did Harley forget something?"

"No. I'm here to pick her up." Her heart picked up speed at the seconds that ticked in the silence between them.

"Let me call Mrs. Norton down at aftercare. One moment please." The receptionist turned in her chair and phoned the room.

Sarah drummed her nails on the counter with impatience. A flutter of fear settled in her chest alongside her racing heart. "What's going on?"

"Come with me, Ms. Eastman." The receptionist's heels on the floor echoed in the empty hall. Sarah followed her closely and met Mrs. Norton in the hallway outside Harley's classroom.

"Sarah, hi. I'm sorry, but Harley isn't here."

"What do you mean she isn't here?" Sarah stared at Mrs. Norton's trembling lips, and that was when the panic settled into her bones. Her daughter was missing. "How long has she been missing?"

"It was crazy at dismissal time. Matthew got sick, and while I was tending to him, Harley said you were here, and I let her go. I just did."

"Okay, okay. Let's take a minute. I'm going to call my aunt. Maybe Harley walked home." When her aunt answered, Sarah kept her voice even and calm. "Aunt Judy, are you home? Harley isn't at school and we're trying to find her."

"What do you mean?" Aunt Judy's voice rose in fear.

"Is she home with you?"

"No. I haven't seen her since this morning. She's not at school?"

"I'm here now, and they said she's already left."

"Shit. I'm on my way. You'd better call Natalie. She'll know what to do," Judy said.

Sarah shook her head at the two women staring at her. "Good idea. I'll do that." Sarah hung up the phone and dialed Nat's number.

"Sheriff Strand."

"Nat. It's Sarah. I need you. Harley's missing."

CHAPTER THIRTEEN

Natalie had handled missing-children cases before with a hundred percent success rate. Children got lost in the woods every year. They had a system of what to do first and who to call. Hearing the raw panic in Sarah's voice made Natalie forget everything for about five seconds until her training kicked in. "Where are you?"

"At the school."

"I'll be right there." She took a deep breath and called Faith, keeping the information off the radio for now. "Sarah's daughter Harley left school unattended. I'm headed there now to see if we can pull up video. Have everyone on standby if we need to start a search."

She hung up and briskly walked to her car. Not sweet Harley. Not her. Natalie had a protocol to follow, and her mind immediately went to Francine. It was too coincidental that the one day she showed up, Harley ended up missing. She flipped on her lights and drove as fast and as carefully as she could. She was at the school in less than two minutes.

"I don't know what to do." Sarah walked into Natalie's arms and cried the moment Natalie pulled her close.

Natalie held Sarah to offer comfort in a moment of free-falling. She dried her tears and looked into her eyes. "We're going to find her. She couldn't have gotten far. What time does school let out?"

"Three thirty," Mrs. Norton said.

"We need to look at all the video from all the cameras to see if we can locate her. So, you think she left at three thirty or around dismissal time?"

Mrs. Norton nodded. "Yes. Matthew was sick, and she said her mom was here."

Natalie turned to Sarah. "Call Francine. See if she's with her. Maybe she took her out for ice cream or early dinner." While Sarah made the call, Natalie asked to see all recordings on all the cameras at dismissal. Principal Mickey Greer showed up right as they pulled up the videos. She shook his hand and told him everything she knew.

"Whatever you need." He nodded at her.

Mickey and Natalie had history that wasn't pretty when they were teenagers, but they had grown to respect one another since she returned home. People grew up and out of their former shells, so she left the past where it was. "Pull up the camera at the front of the school and the parking lot. Check cars. Sarah, what kind of car was Francine driving?"

"Could this be a kidnapping? Do we need to call the FBI?" Mickey asked.

"Let's look at the video first. Any luck, Sarah?"

"I can't reach her. It's going to voice mail."

"Did she say what conference and where?" Natalie bit the inside of her cheeks as she waited for Sarah to dig in her brain for the information.

"I honestly didn't pay attention."

Natalie clicked her radio. "Faith. Find any medical conventions happening in Portland. Sports medicine, if it's specialized. Have Joshua drive around and look for any child in a purple coat, jeans, and pink shirt who is unattended anywhere. I'll text you a photo in a minute." She waited for Faith to confirm before returning her attention to the cameras. She reached back and held Sarah's hand. "We'll find her."

They pulled up videos from all the exits and watched. When they found her on the camera, the energy changed from fear to excitement. "Pull up the playground." They watched as she approached a cat near the edge of the woods and followed it in.

Sarah reached out at the camera. "No, baby. That's not Salem."

"You have a cat?" Natalie asked.

"Francine has a black cat named Salem, and it was very hard for Harley to say good-bye. She probably thinks that stray cat is him." Sarah groaned.

"We have a starting point." Natalie told Mickey to keep watching the monitor and stepped away to call in reinforcements. School was going to be base camp because it had plenty of room and lights. Faith called in the volunteers, and within twenty minutes, Natalie was organizing a search. Several teachers who were familiar with the outskirts of the woods started searching. "Nobody leaves by themselves. It's getting dark, and I don't want to have to add names to the list. Everyone has a picture of the child. Grab a radio and check in."

"I need to get out there, Natalie. I need to find her."

Sarah looked so helpless and vulnerable. It crushed Natalie's soul to see her so broken. "You need to stay here, because when they find her, she's going to want you right away. You don't know these woods, Sarah. I can't have you getting lost, too. I'm only letting the people who have experience doing this out there. It's already dusk, and the woods are bad enough in daylight."

"Anything yet?"

Judy and Bob showed up, along with four veterans from the lodge. Judy hugged Sarah and looked at Natalie hopefully.

"Nothing yet, but we can use all the help we can get. Grab a flashlight and a walkie and help if you can." She eyed the oldest, who probably hovered around seventy, and asked him to stay with Judy and Sarah while they went out. "I need somebody who can be my point of contact with the mother. Will you be that person?" He nodded, and she handed him a walkie.

Natalie figured they had at least two dozen people out in the dark looking for Harley. Faith had the exact count. Everyone knew it wasn't safe to be in the woods at night, so the teachers pulled back and patrolled the town instead. Sawyer sent over a team of search and rescue to continue looking in the forest. They were trained for those maneuvers. The temperature was forecast to drop dangerously low. Natalie contacted Oregon's highway patrol and asked for the K-9 units. They were in northern Oregon looking for lost hikers, but a unit would be there in the morning.

"Judy, maybe somebody should be at home in case she shows up there. Even though she doesn't know the town, she'll recognize familiar places," Natalie said.

Bob spoke up. "You stay here. I'll go home and look around. She might be scared or hiding."

Thank God, because his pacing was driving Natalie crazy. His anxiety wasn't helping the situation at all. It was time for one of them to go. Natalie looked at her watch. It was almost seven, and the temperature had dropped several degrees when the sun set. Every time she looked at Sarah, her heart broke a little more. She had to get out there and help find Harley. When Gravy's showed up with warm food for the volunteers, Natalie decided to make her move. "Things are under control here. I'm going to grab a few things I have at the house and join the search. Call me on the walkie if you need me, but I need you to stay here, Sarah. Promise me." She touched her cheek. As soon as she got the promising nod, she stood and checked in with Faith. "I'll be back."

It took a bit to maneuver out of the parking lot, but she got home within a few minutes. Ghost Dog greeted her happily but paused when he seemed to sense her anxiety. "Hey, buddy. I'm sorry you've been cooped up all afternoon. We have to hurry though. Harley is missing. You know, Sarah's daughter. Let's go outside, and then I'll feed you." She clicked his leash and led him around the yard until he did his business.

While he wolfed down his food, she slipped into warmer weatherproof pants, changed into a warm sweater, and put on her orange safety coat with reflective striping and LED lights. She wore her snake-proof boots because they were warm, almost too warm, and would protect her ankles and shins from undergrowth in the dark. She raced out to the shed, grabbed her headlamp, gloves, and her emergency backpack. She checked her watch. It had been twelve minutes since she got home. Every minute counted when a child was missing. She had to join the search. She couldn't stand around and delegate. Harley was out there alone, and these woods were dark, tricky, and thick. And it was cold.

She turned, and panic set in again. The back door was wide open. She forgot to close it in her haste. "Oh, no!" She raced into the house and yelled and whistled. The house was quiet. Ghost Dog was gone.

❖

"Sheriff. Come in, Sheriff."

Natalie clicked her radio on. She and Matt Miller, a volunteer fire fighter from Sawyer, had been out for two hours.

They had paired up with ten other volunteers who knew the area well and could cover a lot of ground. The search was slow and frustrating. The moon offered very little help, and as much as Natalie didn't want to give up, it was getting too dangerous for the volunteers to be out. She couldn't handle anyone else getting lost. Harley and now Ghost Dog. Her heart couldn't take more. "Sheriff, here. What's going on, Faith?"

"Francine Morris is here."

Her exhaustion evaporated, replaced by anger, jealousy, and fear. Fear that she had something to do with Harley's disappearance. Jealousy because, even though they were no longer a family, Francine was still an anchor in their lives. And anger. If Francine had anything to do with Harley's disappearance, then she feared what she would do to her. As an officer of the law, she had a responsibility to protect and serve, and that was going to be hard. She took a deep breath. "We'll work our way back." She whistled to Matt. "I've got to get back to base." She practically growled.

"You should probably call it, Sheriff."

Natalie bent over as the realization struck her. She wanted to puke. How could she call off a search when a little girl was out there in the cold—scared, all alone? This was the part of her job she hated. These decisions were rare, but they happened. "You're right. It's too dangerous." She had Dr. Martin at base camp to treat minor injuries among the volunteers, and he was having a hard time keeping up, according to Faith. "Five more minutes. Then I'll call it." She couldn't imagine what Sarah was thinking or going through. She and Matt resumed their path, yelling out Harley's name. The darkness was punctuated with beams of light from the dozen volunteers who were skirting the area with them. Natalie's radio hissed to life.

"Sheriff."

"Strand here."

"The volunteers by Hunter's Ridge have a lead."

Natalie held her breath as she waited for the news. A lead meant they had a direction. They could turn their efforts and send more volunteers to the ridge to cover more ground. Maybe calling it now for the night was a mistake. "Go ahead." She heard static and an exhale of breath.

"They found a shoe."

❖

"So, you left Spruce Mountain and drove straight to the Marriott in Portland?" Natalie asked.

"I have no idea why I'm being questioned. I came up here the second I got Sarah's message," Francine said.

Natalie studied Francine's body language. She exhibited all the signs of somebody who was innocent, but Natalie wasn't taking any chances. She was tired and being extra careful. Everyone was tired. It was midnight, and Harley had been missing for almost nine hours.

"I'm just trying to figure out your timeline. I'm not an important doctor or anything, but I check my phone a lot during the day, and I'm wondering why it took you all day and most of the evening to get back to Sarah," Natalie said.

Francine rubbed her hands up and down her pants and stood. She was tall, but Natalie was taller. "Who listens to voice mail anymore?"

"Um, doctors with patients and an answering service?" Natalie knew she needed to keep it professional and reined in her emotions, so she redirected. "I get that you didn't listen to it, but you literally just spent last night with your family."

"As my ex-wife so righteously pointed out, I'm no longer a member of the family. I didn't want to talk to her, so I didn't take her calls or listen to her messages."

"How many times does Sarah have to call you before you take it seriously?"

"It's not a crime to not answer a phone, Sheriff."

Point to Francine. Natalie took a step back and rubbed her hands over her face. "I know you don't like me questioning you, but I'm trying to rule you out, not blame you for anything."

"I gain nothing by taking Harley."

"That's pretty low."

Francine sat back down. "I mean, I wouldn't take her to get back at Sarah. I was an asshole when we were married, and truth be told, I'm glad we're not anymore. I'm not a family-oriented person. I wouldn't want to take Harley. I love her, but I would never destroy Sarah by taking her. I want to find her as much as you all do."

Natalie never told Francine about the video. She assumed somebody had told her, but maybe they hadn't. She asked again about her timeline and went through her day. Nothing really seemed out of the ordinary, so she released her but told her to stay close. She asked for Oregon Highway Patrol's help in confirming Francine's story. Their resources were better.

When she wrapped up, she went to find Sarah, who looked exhausted. "You should try to get some sleep. There are cots in the administration office."

Sarah walked into Natalie's arms. "Please don't make me go. I need to stay here in case they find her."

"*When* they find her," Natalie said. She tilted Sarah's chin so she could look at her eyes. "We will find her." Finding her shoe meant that she was more than likely lost. It meant that somebody hadn't taken her. She was close. Natalie could feel it. They were going to find her, and she was going to be okay.

"Everyone is so kind for helping us. We've only been in town for a short while, and so many people are here to help."

Natalie wiped the tears from Sarah's cheeks. "That's why

living in a small town is a good thing. Everybody cares. Now please get some rest."

"You need to rest, too." Natalie didn't argue. She walked Sarah to Mickey's office and sat with her on the couch. Within a matter of seconds, Sarah was asleep, her head on Natalie's shoulder. The last thing Natalie remembered was reaching for Sarah's hand and entwining their fingers to ensure Sarah felt safe.

❖

"Natalie. Natalie. Wake up."

Natalie woke to Betty shaking her gently. "What's going on? What time is it?" Sarah had slipped down. Her head was in Natalie's lap, which prevented Natalie from jumping up at whatever news Betty had.

"Nothing new, but volunteers are starting to gather because it'll be light in about an hour. I wanted to let you both rest as long as possible."

Natalie tucked a piece of hair behind Sarah's ear. She looked so peaceful, and as much as it pained her to wake her, she knew Sarah would want to be at the front lines waiting for news. "Sarah. Wake up. It's time to get up."

Sarah bolted up. "What? What's happening? Have they found her? What time is it?" She stood and stumbled. Betty grabbed her before she fell.

"No news yet. The other deputies are patrolling the town quickly before they join in the search. We have a lot more volunteers, Sheriff. Sawyer's here, and the highway patrol is twenty minutes out."

"Thanks for waking us up." Natalie stood and did a quick stretch. It was the most uncomfortable sleep she'd ever had. Her entire body was stiff from pushing herself through the woods, tripping and falling repeatedly, then sleeping upright for a few hours. "Let's find out what's going on."

She took Sarah's hand and led her out of the office. She completely understood the hard grasp of Sarah's hand in hers. Uneasiness pricked her, and she couldn't figure out why. Something else was on her mind. She needed to splash her face with water and drink a hot cup of coffee to help her wake up and concentrate harder. The moment she walked into the gym, she remembered. A wave of panic washed over her, filling her with dread. Not only was Harley still missing, but so was Ghost Dog, and it was her fault. She shouldn't have left the damn door open. She took a deep breath and moved to the area where volunteers were congregating. Joshua had maps of the area spread out.

"Where did they find the shoe?" Sarah asked.

Joshua didn't look up as he pointed to a small x on the map. "Three miles from here, but a hard three miles." The volunteers had combed that area last night for a solid hour before the search was called off for the night.

"You can almost mark a straight line from the school to where she went. Let's send eighty percent of the volunteers in that direction. A ten-foot spread between everyone, so if she's asleep or scared, somebody should be able to spot her," Natalie said. She shot Joshua a hard look to remind him to be aware of his audience. He slinked away and pulled together the first wave of volunteers—the people who knew the woods the best.

"Highway called. Once it's light out, they'll fly around the area to see if they can see anything," Betty said.

Natalie wondered if Betty had slept at all. "Doesn't anyone have a drone they could fly? We need to add one to the budget. I just think a loud helicopter is going to scare her, but we'll take what we can get."

She asked Sarah to patiently wait at the school again. She was going out with the first wave and needed to get ready. Her emergency bag still had all the necessities and a few granola bars and water. She slung it over her shoulder, grabbed a fully charged radio, and took off with Matt and two other volunteers from Sawyer. While the rest of the volunteers combed the area around the ridge, Natalie and her crew would head south of the ridge and look for her there. With only one shoe, Harley wouldn't be able to get far.

"We'll check in every half hour," Natalie said. The four flipped on their bright flashlights and entered the dark forest with renewed vigor. They hit the ridge, checked in, and headed south. The sun was finally adding light to their search. "Let's spread out a little more so we can cover more ground." Natalie broke away from the group and listened.

She thought she heard a bark, but it could have been a woodland creature somewhere making noise. She stilled and listened again. The other three in her group were too far away to make noise. She could hear them call out every ten seconds or so, but in the stillness of the early morning, she heard a bark. Then another one. She picked up the pace and raced to the barking noise. She saw Ghost Dog's blondish-reddish fur and smiled. "Come here, boy!" She dropped to her knees and hugged him when he raced to her. He kissed her, then backed away and barked at her. When he ran off she yelled, "Come back here." He stopped and looked at her and barked again. He did it again before she finally caught on. He wanted her to follow him.

She ran toward him, and every time she got close, he ran faster. He always stayed ahead. "This better not be a game." In her heart, she knew it wasn't. Hope filled her as she got closer to him. This time, he didn't run away when she reached him. She slowed and watched him walk over to a hollowed-out tree that had fallen some time ago. Tucked inside, still sleeping, was Harley. She was dirty and unkempt, but breathing softly. Ghost Dog curled up in front of Harley and rested his head by hers. Natalie dropped to her knees and burst into tears.

CHAPTER FOURTEEN

They found her!"

Sarah jumped up from the chair and ran over to Faith, who had hollered out the announcement.

"Is she okay?" Sarah clutched Faith's arm and waited for more information.

Faith put her hand on Sarah's hand. "She's fine. Natalie's with her, and they are headed back here." She did a call-all and announced Harley was safe and all volunteers should return to base.

Sarah sat down and cried. Aunt Judy rubbed her back and cried with her. These were the good tears. "She's fine. I can't believe it. I can't believe it," Judy said.

"I knew she would be. She's resilient, like her mother," Francine said.

Sarah grabbed Francine's hand. "Thank you for coming back. I know you were busy this week."

"Stop. This is way more important than any conference."

"When will they be here?" Sarah asked.

"Probably in about twenty minutes or so. The sheriff and her crew covered a lot of ground this morning. We can't get to them until they reach a clearing," Faith said.

"Ms. Eastman? Ma'am? I'm going to take a car and head

over to where they should be exiting the woods. Would you like to come with me?" David asked.

"Yes. Please."

When all of them jumped up, David blushed and apologized. "I can fit only one person. The rest of you will have to wait here. We'll be back in a flash."

Sarah hugged Aunt Judy and Francine. "Call Uncle Bob and let him know we have her."

"Good idea. Go, baby. Bring her back to us," Aunt Judy said.

"We'll go out the back. It's where I parked the van."

"Why the van?"

"We have the sheriff, your daughter, three other volunteers who were with Natalie, and a dog."

"Wait. A dog? Natalie's dog?"

"You mean Ghost Dog? I don't know. She just requested the van," David said.

Sarah dug her nails into her hands to keep from reaching over and driving for David. He was extremely cautious and slow. He rounded a corner, slowed down, and finally pulled over. He pointed to a clearing. "They should be coming from that trail, but I don't know for sure."

Sarah stayed glued to her seat with her eyes on the small opening in the woods. When she saw Ghost Dog, she opened the door and ran to him. The rest of the volunteers were close behind. "Baby! My baby! Harley." She couldn't even form complete sentences. She reached for Harley, who started crying the minute she saw Sarah.

"She's fine. I gave her a granola bar and some water, but we're going to take her to the hospital in Sawyer and have her checked out."

Sarah held Harley as tight as she could. "You're okay,

baby. You're home. You're home." She looked over Harley's shoulder and thanked the volunteers for finding her.

"Let's go. I want to get her warmer than she is." Natalie had wrapped Harley in her jacket and put a glove on the foot where she'd lost her shoe. "We'll drop everyone off at the school before we head to the hospital."

"Sweetheart, what happened?" Sarah clutched her close and waited for Harley's tears to subside.

"I don't know." She repeated the same thing until Sarah gave up. They would get the story out of her soon enough.

❖

"She's fine. They're giving her an IV just as a precaution. She's wrapped in a warming blanket and feeling like her old self," Sarah said.

"Can I see her?" Francine asked. "I'll be quick."

Sarah figured Francine would hit the road sooner if she got to see Harley first. "I'll take you back there." Their exchange took less than five minutes. Francine told her how brave she was and not to ever scare them like that again. She kissed Harley's forehead and said she would call her later in the week. And just like that, she was gone again. "Natalie, Harley wants you."

Natalie followed Sarah and stopped when Sarah turned in front of Harley's door.

Sarah placed her hand on Natalie's arm. "She asked for you first, but I wanted to get Francine out of here. I hope you understand that." When Natalie nodded but still hadn't smiled, Sarah stepped closer and pulled Natalie into a hug. They held one another for several moments. "Thank you so much for finding her. You told me you would, and you did." Sarah brushed the tears from her own cheeks and kissed Natalie swiftly. "Thank you."

"You are most certainly welcome. Now can I see her?"

Sarah opened the door. "Harley, look who's here."

"Sheriff Natalie. Hi." Harley raised up her pink bunny that Uncle Bob had brought from home.

"I bet you're glad to be in a warm bed, huh?"

Harley nodded. "I was cold last night."

"Looks like you're going to be able to go home right after lunch," Natalie said.

"Do I have to go to school?" Harley and Natalie both looked at Sarah, waiting for an answer.

"No, baby. You get to stay home today and maybe tomorrow. We have to see what the doctor recommends."

"Can I see Henry?"

"Who's Henry?" Sarah tried hard not to freak out. She didn't know a Henry, and she hoped to God Harley hadn't met a Henry in the woods.

"The dog who stayed with me."

"Did he stay with you all night?" Natalie asked.

Harley nodded. "He kept me warm."

"You called him Henry," Natalie said.

"That's the name I heard." Harley shrugged. Her little shoulders barely lifted the oversized hospital gown.

"Did somebody say his name?" Sarah asked. Fear struck deep inside at the thought of somebody being alone with her child.

"No. Not really. I just heard it."

"But you didn't see anybody, right?" Natalie asked.

Harley huffed. "Nobody was there. Only Henry."

Sarah cupped her cheek. "It's okay. We can talk about it later."

"I'll be right back," Natalie said.

While Natalie excused herself, Sarah texted Aunt Judy and Uncle Bob and told them to come to Harley's room.

"Harley, we were so worried." Aunt Judy rocked Harley and kissed her forehead. "You can't do that again."

"I won't. I promised Mom already."

Uncle Bob, careful of her IV, sat on the other side of the bed and hugged her when Aunt Judy was done. Sarah loved watching their exchange. It was exactly what she wanted for Harley. Roots. Safety. A home. Sarah sat back but refused to get comfortable. It would be too easy to drop from exhaustion right now, and they still had to get home.

"Why did you leave the school?" Aunt Judy asked.

Harley tucked her head against Aunt Judy's shoulder—a sign she was embarrassed. As much as she loved attention, this wasn't the good kind, and everyone knew it.

"You were following that cat who looked like Salem, huh?" Sarah asked. Harley nodded but didn't look up. Sarah had thought Harley knew better than to chase or follow any animal. "Salem is back in Texas, sweetie. You can't just leave school for any reason. I want you to promise me you'll stay in school and not leave unless somebody who is approved picks you up, okay? You scared a lot of people. They practically shut down the town to make sure you were safe." The last thing Sarah wanted to do was scold Harley, especially in the hospital, but Harley needed to know that what she did was unacceptable, and there were consequences to her actions. She didn't get far because the door opened slowly, and Ghost Dog and Natalie walked in.

"Henry!" Harley yelled and reached for him. Much to everyone's surprise, he jumped on the bed and crawled up to kiss her cheeks. "What are you doing here?"

"How'd you sneak him in here?" Sarah petted his soft fur.

"I'm the sheriff. I'm kind of a big deal around here,"

Natalie said. "He's so gentle that I said he was Harley's hero and maybe a therapy dog. He's so incredibly sweet with her. Look at them."

Sarah teared up at their tender exchange. "How did he find her? How did he know to even look for her?"

"I wonder if he understood me or felt my mood and knew something bad had happened. The door was barely open when I went out to the workshop to get my emergency backpack."

She felt Natalie entwine their fingers and smiled for the first time. "I know you struggled to find him, but I'm so happy he got away. Without him, we'd probably still be looking for Harley."

"He's very special. He came into our lives for a reason. I'm going to take him home and make sure he's good. Call you later?" Natalie asked.

Sarah watched as Natalie tried hard to convince Henry to go with her. She smiled as Natalie reasoned with him and promised they would visit Harley soon. He slowly climbed down and looked back at Harley several times before they left. She couldn't blame him. Her daughter was the most important person in the world. "I'll take care of her, Henry. I promise you can see her tomorrow."

❖

"I want to go to school, Mom."

Sarah cracked her eyes open to find Harley leaning over her. "What time is it?" She turned her head to check the clock. "Harley Nicole. It's five thirty in the morning. Go back to bed or come here." She pulled back the blanket and patted the small area beside her.

Harley giggled and snuggled next to Sarah. "Mom, are you still mad at me?"

"I was never mad at you. I was scared that somebody took you," Sarah said. She gave Harley another hug and said a quick prayer of thanks that her daughter had been found alive, healthy, and unharmed.

"Henry took care of me."

"Did Henry just show up, or what happened?" She smoothed down Harley's hair and placed several baby kisses on her temple. This was the perfect way to have a conversation.

"I don't know. It got dark and I sat on a tree and Henry was just there. I got tired, and he cuddled with me like we're doing. Only he's a dog."

"He's a big dog, and he kept you warm and safe." Sarah paused and continued to stroke Harley's hair. "So, you heard a voice tell you his name?"

Harley shrugged. "I don't know if it was a person. I just heard the name, and he likes it. I mean, every time I said it, he came to me."

"Did he leave you ever?"

"When I woke up, he was there with Sheriff Natalie." Harley pressed her palm against Sarah's as she talked.

Sarah loved it when Harley held her hand up to her own as they snuggled. Her daughter was incredible. "What do you think of Sheriff Natalie? Do you like her?"

"She's really nice. I didn't get to ride in her car yesterday. Do you think she'll take me tomorrow?"

"Sheriff Natalie will definitely take you to school this week. She was very excited to take you yesterday, but Francine wanted to," Sarah said.

"Why did Francine come?"

Good question, Sarah thought. "To say hello. She had a conference for her work in Portland and thought she would stop and visit. It was nice of her, right?"

Harley nodded. "I like Sheriff Natalie a lot."

"I do, too. Now let's get some sleep because it is way too early for this. It's not even light out. Close your eyes." Within two minutes, Harley was asleep. Sarah snuggled under the covers holding her daughter close, vowing to never lose sight of her again.

Five hours later, they were still in bed, but Sarah didn't care. She knew Mary was fine with her taking the day off, given the circumstances. When Harley started stirring, Sarah woke her up gently. "Are you hungry? Maybe some pancakes?"

Harley made tiny mewling noises until Sarah poked her awake. She played grumpy for about ten seconds until Sarah mentioned pancakes again, and then she started to smile. Her single dimple made Sarah melt. "Meet me upstairs in ten minutes. Don't fall back to sleep or I'll have Uncle Bob bring you upstairs, and you don't want that."

Harley sat up. "I want to go with you."

Sarah offered her back, and Harley whooped once and jumped on. "Ugh. I really have to stop carrying you. You're almost as tall as I am." Harley wasn't going to be tall, but she would for sure tower above her five-four frame.

"Mom's making pancakes." Harley climbed off Sarah's back and hugged Aunt Judy.

"It's almost lunchtime," Aunt Judy said.

"Who says you can't have pancakes for lunch? Today is a free day, so we can do what we want, when we want," Sarah said.

"Good point. Bob and I just ate. We didn't want to wake you because you both needed sleep."

"I think we're caught up now. Thanks for letting us sleep in."

"What are your plans for today?"

"I want to see Henry," Harley said.

"I guess see Henry and take treats over to the sheriff's

department." The need to see Natalie was incredibly strong. Hugging and kissing would be icing on the cake, but just to see her was what she wanted most. "I probably need to check in with Mary. I think tomorrow we'll get back on schedule."

"I'd recommend taking one of the thousands of desserts people ran over last night to Bob. They're on the counter." Aunt Judy nodded over in the direction of the counter closest to the pantry.

"Oh, my gosh. That's a ton of food." Sarah held up banana-nut bread from the Wilsons, pumpkin bread from Mike and Carly Blantz, cookies from Creative Crafts, fruit cake from Jim and Nancy Pierce. There was homemade soup from the Robinsons, a quiche from Amanda Pritz, and fresh eggs and cheese from the Bradfords.

"There are three casseroles downstairs in the freezer."

"Wow. We won't have to cook for a long time. I'll definitely grab a bagful of stuff for Natalie and the department." She turned to Harley. "You still want pancakes?"

"Can we have pancakes and cookies?"

Sarah pretended to think long and hard about her question. "How about you eat your pancakes and then have a cookie? You don't want to eat too much and get sick when we visit Natalie and Henry, do you?"

"Okay. One pancake and one cookie?"

"I can live with that."

CHAPTER FIFTEEN

Everything about organizing a successful search and rescue was gratifying except the mounds of paperwork that had to be filled out afterward. Natalie was on her couch after she and Henry had a much-needed nap. Henry. That was a name she was going to have to get used to. Like Harley said, he seemed very accustomed to it, so it probably was his name. How Harley had heard the name was completely out of the realm of logic. It gave her the creeps really. She didn't believe in ghosts or spirits, but this whole thing made her rethink her beliefs. "Henry." She whispered his name. He immediately turned his head and looked up at her. "So, no more Ghost Dog for you. Or buddy. Just Henry." He wagged his tail against the couch cushion.

That was his favorite place—on the couch sprawled next to her. He always had to have a part of his body touching her. His paw, his head, his ribs. Even if she moved slightly, he adjusted so they were always touching. "I really wonder where you came from." She rubbed his stomach and watched as he closed his eyes. He trusted her completely, and the feeling was reciprocated. Now she wasn't sure she wanted to find his real owner. Maybe they had dumped him or he'd escaped for a reason. Not everyone loved dogs, because they required a lot of attention and people got in over their heads. It wasn't her place to judge them. She hated taking animals to the animal shelter in Sawyer, but it happened. "Not you, big boy. You're staying here if you want." Another tail wag.

Somebody is dying to see Henry. Are you at work?

Natalie snapped a picture of Henry on his back looking up at the camera.

No, we took the day off. Come over if you want.

We took the day off, too.

Natalie held her breath. It was the first time she'd had a picture of both of them.

Your mini-me for sure.

We have several loaves of sweet stuff if you're hungry. We can bring that over.

I'm sure I could eat something.

Natalie wasn't hungry. Her stomach still burned from the entire ordeal. She had almost lost a kid on her watch. Not just any kid, but the child of a woman she wanted a relationship with. And Harley was such a sweet girl. Very smart, not spoiled, and she genuinely cared about so many different things. She had shown so much trust when Natalie gently woke her up. Harley had blinked a few times and clutched Natalie's neck as tight as she could when Natalie scooped her up. Once she'd realized she was safe, she cried. They both had.

Natalie had radioed Matt, who was the closest volunteer to her. He had found them both and walked ahead clearing a path. Henry hadn't been happy when Matt showed up. Natalie didn't think he would leave them, but she'd still worried about his safety. When he had jumped into the van, she'd breathed a sigh of relief. She didn't know if she had the energy to go back out for another search-and-rescue mission right on the heels of Harley's.

"Okay, Henry. Guess what? We are having guests, so we need to straighten up the place. I think you're going to like who's coming over." Natalie got up and applied a light layer of makeup, brushed her hair back into a ponytail, and slipped on jeans and a sweater. She found fun, fuzzy, no-slip socks and even a cute pumpkin bandana that she put around Henry's neck.

"Henry!"

Natalie turned to find Harley standing in the foyer hugging Henry. "Hi."

"Oh, my God. I'm so sorry, Nat. I sent her ahead of me, but I didn't realize she was going to rudely barge in." Sarah put her hands on her hips. "What do you say?"

"I'm sorry. I was so excited to see Henry again."

Natalie waved them off. While it surprised her, she found it was a very comfortable feeling knowing that Harley felt safe here. "No worries. The door is always unlocked."

"Even at night?" Harley asked.

Natalie was careful about answering. "It's better to lock doors at night. And probably during the day, too." She knelt to have direct contact with Harley, who was too busy loving on Henry to give her full attention to anything. "And I have a very smart, loyal dog who lives here, who can protect me if somebody bad tries to come into my house."

"And you're the sheriff."

"This is true."

"So that makes this a safe place."

Harley's logic made Natalie laugh. She stood and looked at Sarah. "You have a future lawyer on your hands. Hi. Come on in." She reached over and took the heavy bag from Sarah's hand. In a move that surprised both of them, Sarah kissed her. It was swift and sweet and right in front of Harley.

"Hi. We're here."

"I see that. What goodies did you bring me?" Natalie lifted her eyebrow at Sarah, who rewarded her with a wink.

"Um, we have pumpkin bread and some lemon bars. And a casserole from the post office."

Since Natalie hadn't gotten to eat any of the pumpkin bread her mother had made, she reached for that first. "I usually hate everything pumpkin by Thanksgiving. Thankfully, we have three weeks before that."

"What are you doing for Thanksgiving?" Sarah asked.

"Usually Mom and I just cook a nice meal and hang out."

"Come over. Let's all have Thanksgiving at the house. Aunt Judy and Uncle Bob would love the company," Sarah said.

Natalie couldn't say no to Sarah if she tried. "I'll check with Mom, but I'm sure it'll be okay. She'll want to bring dessert."

"We'll take care of the savory stuff, and you take care of the sweet stuff. Deal?"

"Sounds perfect."

"Where are Henry's toys?" Harley asked. She looked around the living room and by his bed.

"He doesn't have any toys. Yet," Natalie added. knowing full well they would have to remedy that situation quickly.

"Why not?"

"Well, I was hoping we would find his owners soon."

"He doesn't have anybody anymore," Harley said.

He offered her a paw, and she shook it. Then he rolled over when Harley made a twirling motion with her finger.

"Hold up. This dog knows tricks?" Natalie completely blew over the part about Henry not having family. Harley knowing his name, or at least a name he was familiar with, was already over the top. She couldn't take any more.

"Honey, did he tell you he doesn't have a family anymore?" Sarah asked.

"Don't be silly. He can't talk."

"Then how do you know he doesn't have one?"

Harley grew quiet. "I just do. I don't know how. Can I take him outside and play with him?"

Natalie looked at Henry. "Are you going to be a good boy and stay in the yard, or do you want to go on the leash?"

"Let's put him on the leash. That way neither one of them gets away." Sarah's suggestion had merit.

"Do you know how to walk a dog?" Natalie asked.

Harley laughed and nodded.

"You'd be surprised how many people don't know. Here are the rules. Stay in the yard. Don't go past the shed. And don't step in anything." Natalie crinkled her nose for effect, which made Harley laugh even harder. She tethered Henry to the leash and gave the handle to Harley. "Nobody gets lost today. Don't let him push you around, and if he jerks you and tries to get away, just drop the leash. I don't want you to get hurt. You have five minutes. Make them count." Natalie zipped up Harley's jacket and opened the back door for them.

"You're so good with children," Sarah said.

Natalie barely had the door closed before Sarah was in her arms, kissing her. This one wasn't the sweet, gentle kiss of new lovers, but it was a passionate one that she felt was long overdue. She kissed her back with as much desperation as she felt. If Harley hadn't been there, there would've been a trail of clothes leading back to Natalie's bed. "I've missed you." Natalie broke the kiss and looked out the window. Seeing that Harley and Henry were safe and playing, Natalie turned her attention to Sarah but took a step back. Now wasn't the time. "How are you holding up?"

"I'm okay. I probably aged ten years and need more sleep, but I'm just so thankful she's home."

Natalie tilted Sarah's chin up. "You look beautiful." She liked the way Sarah averted her eyes and blushed whenever she received a compliment. "Even after such a horrible ordeal."

"No parent should have to go through that. Is it legal to chip your kid?" Sarah asked.

Natalie laughed at first and then gave the question more thought. "I'm sure they have trackers you can put on their clothes or in backpacks. That might be a worthwhile investment, especially after what you just went through."

"Maybe you need one for Henry, too. They probably have something you can attach to his collar, like a GPS chip. I mean, if you're thinking of keeping him."

"According to Harley, he doesn't have a family. We could share him. You get him on the weekends, I get him during the week, or something like that."

"That actually sounds like a great idea." Sarah looked out the window and watched Henry and Harley play. "They obviously have a very strong connection, and keeping them apart would be a mistake."

"Keeping us apart would be a big mistake. We obviously have a very strong connection, too," Natalie said. She pulled Sarah into another embrace and kissed her slowly. She shivered when she felt Sarah's hands under her sweater, stroking her back softly.

"We've had a strong connection since we were teenagers. I can't believe I didn't act on my crush."

"Technically, you did. There was some pretty fantastic kissing at that party. You were bold back then."

Sarah hid her face in her hands. "I still can't believe I did that."

Natalie gently pulled Sarah's hands down and entwined their fingers. "Best night of my life."

"Best?"

Natalie put her forefinger on her bottom lip and looked up as though she was giving the question the most thought she could. She nodded. "Best so far."

"Better than the other night? Right over there on that couch?"

"The one where you sneaked away in the middle of the night and I woke up shirtless and alone?"

Another blush spread across Sarah's features. "Ack. Stop."

"I'm teasing. I'm sure we have plenty more nights together. Hopefully in the very near future." One more kiss and then she would call in Harley and Henry.

"Okay, you two. Come on in. It's cold out there." Sarah opened the door and waved them in.

"He needs a toy, Mom." Harley walked Henry in and unclipped his leash and handed it to Natalie.

"Thank you," Natalie said. She put the leash up. "And you're right. He needs toys. Maybe if you two aren't busy, we can take him to the big animal stores outside of Portland and pick out a few things."

"Maybe this weekend? And in the meantime, we can pick up a toy at Spruce Market. They have a decent selection."

"Can we go now? And bring Henry?" Harley asked.

Another Eastman she couldn't say no to. She was looking for her keys before Sarah interrupted her.

"Why don't we sit down and eat something first. I think we all should just chill for a bit. I brought over something that could be zucchini bread or banana bread, and I even have a casserole in the bag. Maybe we can do an early dinner?"

"I think time with the both of you sounds perfect," Natalie said. It surprised her that she meant it, but her feelings for both of them had grown exponentially since Harley had gone missing. And it had been less than forty-eight hours. Sarah was right. Everyone was still emotionally charged from the last two days, and downtime was exactly what they needed. She watched Harley and Henry snuggle and play, and it was so adorable it nearly made her cry. It took a lot to make her cry. Finding Harley had broken her. Since then, she was emotional about everything.

"Is it weird that we're eating dinner at four thirty?" Sarah asked.

"Based on the average age of the people of Spruce Mountain, this is an appropriate time to eat dinner."

Natalie was rewarded with a friendly shoulder bump from Sarah.

"I can't tell you how tired I am. I would think she would be exhausted, but she's been running full-steam-ahead since she woke up this morning," Sarah said.

"Well, most of your energy was zapped from nerves and fear. I'm surprised you're out and about today."

"I wanted to see you."

Natalie saw the raw need in Sarah's eyes. Without thinking, she pulled Sarah into her embrace and held her close. "I'm so happy you did. Look at them. I still can't believe what happened. How? Why? It's amazing. The whole thing."

"Still no answer on the website? Nobody's come forward?"

"Nope, and honestly, at this point, after everything that's happened, I kind of hope nobody does. If Harley says he doesn't have a home, I'm just going to go with it," Natalie said.

"He belongs with us."

Natalie tried hard to figure out what "us" meant. Were they a thing now? Was Sarah ready to commit? Just a few days ago she was in limbo about the relationship and told Natalie she wanted to go slow. She'd felt Sarah pull away that night.

"I agree. I'll have Sly Stone pull the post. Looks like we have a dog."

The squeal from Harley was expected, but the squeeze and squeal from Sarah weren't. She wrapped her arms around Natalie's waist, and she kissed her shoulder.

"Well, welcome to the family, Henry," Natalie said.

As if he understood, he trotted over to Natalie and licked her hand. Sarah squatted down and hugged him.

"Thank you so much for finding my baby, you brave boy."

Natalie watched the exchange and teared up again. Damn. When was she ever going to stop crying?

CHAPTER SIXTEEN

Sarah checked her watch again. It felt like the longest week on record, followed by painfully slow hours until her date with Natalie. They saw each other a few times the rest of the week, but she either had Harley with her or Natalie was with Linda. There were a few passionate kisses when nobody was looking, but she was aching for time alone with Natalie. This time she wasn't going to stop. She was still kicking herself about that night. Natalie had been nothing but kind and careful with her. Truthfully, she had stopped because her feelings for Natalie were incredibly overwhelming so soon after her divorce. Deep down, she knew she didn't want to leave Spruce Mountain. This was a great town for Harley, especially now that everyone knew them, and Harley loved it. Her classroom was small but challenging, and education meant everything to Sarah. Opening her own business here in town made sense.

"You have two packages today, Sarah," Phil said.

Sarah rubbed her hands together when Phil handed her two small parcels and a few pieces of mail.

"I made it just in time." The post office closed at noon on Saturdays. Harley was in gymnastics across the street, so to kill time, Sarah checked her post-office box. It made her nervous to leave Harley, but Harley enjoyed gymnastics, and it was time to get her back on her schedule. Missing school two days this week had made Harley cranky and whiny. Sarah was hesitant, but after several lengthy discussions, she finally believed Harley when she said she would never leave the school grounds or lie again about an adult picking her up. Her disappearance had shaken them both up. She noticed Harley stood closer when they were out in public. And she had crawled into her bed twice this week.

"Have a nice afternoon," Phil said.

She remembered him from the search. "Thank you again for doing everything to help find Harley. I really appreciate it."

He grumbled and nodded at her, but Sarah could have sworn his chest puffed out a bit. She was starting to like the people in this town. Once Harley was done with gymnastics, she drove home and dropped the boxes on the kitchen table. "Go change your clothes right now." The last thing she needed was to have to buy more leotards. Harley raced downstairs without a reminder. That was another result of getting lost. She did things without questioning everything.

"Oh, Christmas shopping already?" Aunt Judy pointed to the small boxes on the table.

Shit. Sarah was going to have to start thinking about that, too. "No, but I'm excited to open them." She took the scissors from Aunt Judy and opened the smaller box. She pulled out a business card and handed it to Aunt Judy. "The first one is yours."

"I'm so proud of you for doing this. Wanting to stay here in Spruce Mountain. And with your experience and education, you'll have customers in no time." Aunt Judy flipped Sarah's card over and beamed with pride.

"I'll start dropping them off at places in town like the library."

"I'll have Bob leave some at the lodge. I'm sure you'll get

business right away. Oh, and the post office and the bulletin board at Spruce Market. Brian Denmore will have to work a little harder because you're going to steal away all of his business."

Sarah put her hand up to her heart. Today was an overwhelming kind of day. She had made several life-changing decisions in the span of a week.

"What's in the other box?" Aunt Judy shook the box like she would a present, trying to guess its contents.

"It's a tracker for Harley. I'm going to put it in her coat. I was thinking her backpack, but she doesn't always take her bag with her. She hates being cold, so I know she'll always have her coat with her. I'll have to figure something out in summer, but we have some time. Is it too Big Brotherish?"

"Not at all. You're being a parent, and after what just happened, I don't blame you. How does it work?"

Sarah explained the app and how she could use her phone to locate Harley. "She's too young for a cell phone, or else I would just use the tracker on that. And I got one for Natalie and Henry. She's going to put it on his collar."

"You two seem pretty tight. Are you excited about your date tonight?"

It was as if Aunt Judy could read Sarah's mind. She smiled and nodded. "I'm looking forward to adult time. Thanks again for looking after Harley."

"I'm pretty sure Henry will be the one entertaining her tonight."

Natalie made a cute trade with Harley. Harley could have an evening with Henry, if Harley gave her an evening with her mom. Naturally, Harley had jumped at the opportunity. Henry would be dropped off at seven for movie night with Harley and Bob. And if things went her way, Natalie would pick him up early in the morning. "He's wonderful. Thank you for letting him stay here."

"That dog is a hero and can sleep in our bed if he wants," Aunt Judy said.

"I know what you mean. Nat and I joked about splitting our time with him, but I think it's probably going to happen that way. I didn't think Harley was responsible enough with a pet, but oh my gosh, she's so good with him," Sarah said.

"Go relax for a bit. I'll get lunch started for Harley."

Sarah thanked her aunt. She couldn't decide if she needed a nap or to run a marathon. She went downstairs to check on Harley. She was impressed because Harley had taken off her gymnastics uniform and was putting on warmer clothes.

"Mom, can Henry stay the night?"

Sarah sprawled out on Harley's bed. She didn't want to tell her that was the plan all along. "Maybe. We'll have to check with Aunt Judy and Natalie. You know, soon we're going to get our own place, and he can come stay the night whenever we want."

"What's wrong with living here?"

"It's not ours. When we find a house, we can paint and decorate your room however you want."

Harley hopped on the bed next to her. "Will Henry get his own room, too?"

Sarah cupped Harley's chin. "You don't want him to sleep in your bed?"

"Well, yeah, but he needs his own room, too."

Sarah laughed. "No. When we have Henry, he can stay in your room with you. Remember, he's not ours."

"But Sheriff Natalie stopped looking, remember? So that means he's ours."

"Technically, hers. We will just have him on the weekends or whenever we want."

"I want him every day."

Sarah pushed Harley's hair out of her face. "I know, baby. Let's just see how it goes, okay?"

❖

"I'm here for the trade."

Natalie's voice boomed in the house. Harley squealed and raced up the stairs. She crashed into Henry, who greeted her with just as much enthusiasm.

"Hey, hey. Let the poor dog breathe. You're choking him," Sarah said.

Harley released her grip on him and, much to the surprise of everyone in the room, hugged Natalie. "You're early."

Natalie knelt. "Henry couldn't wait to see you, and I couldn't wait to see both of you."

Sarah felt her heart tumble in her chest and drop to her stomach. "Hi."

"Hi. You look great."

Sarah had chosen wool pants this time, a cream-colored cashmere sweater, and boots. She felt great and looked even better. Her hair fell in just the right way, her makeup was perfect, and her outfit made her feel sexy. The look Natalie gave her made her feel invincible. "Thanks. I see Henry has his own overnight bag."

Natalie held up a little duffel bag that read *Spruce Mountain Sheriff's Department* on the side. "It has his favorite toy, food, and some snacks. And his own water dish. First overnight. I'm a little nervous."

Sarah smiled. "You did good. I don't think Henry will be homesick. I understand they will be watching *Moana* and eating popcorn most of the evening."

"No butter on your popcorn," Natalie said. She pointed

at Henry, who only wagged his tail slowly and looked completely unthreatened. "The snacks should tide him over until breakfast."

"He's staying! Woohoo! Come on, Henry. Let's go into the living room."

Sarah gave Harley a quick kiss. "Have fun. Be sure to let him out to go to the bathroom. Remember, he can't tell you when he has to go." She turned to Natalie and whispered, "Or maybe he can. Who knows?"

Natalie threw her hands up. "I'm not questioning anything anymore when it comes to this magical dog. Are you ready to go?"

Sarah blushed and cleared her throat. "I am."

"Have a good night, ladies. We have everything under control here. Don't worry about a thing."

Natalie held the door open for Sarah and followed her out into the cold evening.

"So, Nat, what do you have planned for us? You told me to dress warmly. Keep in mind that this girl has lived in Texas for the last seventeen years. You're going to have to make it worth my while if you're going to keep me out in the elements."

"Let me show you."

The drive to Natalie's house took five minutes. Everything in Spruce Mountain was five minutes away. The grocery store, the market, the school. It was nice. Natalie parked the car, took Sarah's hand, and walked with her to the back of the house, not inside it.

"Oh, my gosh. This is so perfect." Sarah watched as Natalie lit the kindling and logs in the fire pit. She spread one blanket on the bench and motioned for Sarah to sit before covering her with another blanket.

"In about three minutes, you will be toasty warm." She slowly kissed Sarah, teasing her with the gentle promise for later. "And I'll be back in two." Natalie disappeared into the house.

Sarah looked at the stars. Even with the fire blazing in front of her, she could still see the stars clearly. It always amazed her how different the night looked here than in Texas.

"Cider, because what's more fall than that?" Natalie carefully handed her a mug of steaming apple cider.

Sarah inhaled cinnamon, nutmeg, and the tartness of the apples and sighed. "This is perfect."

After poking the logs into a more uniform arrangement, Natalie slipped under the blanket with her. "So now that life has settled somewhat from earlier in the week, tell me how you're doing."

"Surprisingly, I'm at peace. My life is calm here. And a lot of things became very clear to me this week."

"Really? Like what?"

"I like Spruce Mountain. I like the people, I like how everyone came together to help find Harley. I like the slow pace of this town. I thought I would hate it, but it's teaching me to appreciate all things. I even like grumpy old Phil Murphy at the post office."

"Ah, yes. Phil. He's a gentle giant."

"A softie inside."

Natalie laughed. "Oh, let's not get carried away with Phil. What else?"

Sarah gave Natalie her mug to hold and dug around in her coat until she found her business card. "This happened." She took her mug back and handed her card to Natalie.

"You made business cards."

"Yes. I decided to stay and give Spruce Mountain a shot. You and Aunt Judy are right. There is plenty of business in this small town for another CPA. I'll still stay on at the library because it works well with Harley's schedule, but this will give me the extra money I'll need to find a place that Harley and I can call home. We can't live with Aunt Judy and Uncle Bob forever."

Natalie kissed her hard. "That's great. You'll definitely get my business." She put Sarah's fingers up to her neck. "Can you feel how fast my heart is beating at this news?"

It wasn't just the rapid thumping under her fingertips that excited her. It was the smooth, pale skin, the closeness of Natalie's face to hers, and the energy brimming between them. Sarah leaned forward and kissed Natalie. She moaned when she felt Natalie's hand on the back of her neck, holding her close. Sarah ran her tongue over Natalie's bottom lip and sucked it inside her mouth. Their tongues touched gently at first, then with more fervor as their passion ignited. Sarah broke the kiss to put their mugs on the ground and moved closer to Natalie. She kissed her again and straddled Natalie's lap to get closer. "Is this okay?"

Natalie moaned. "This is the best thing ever."

Sarah pulled the blanket over her shoulders to keep them warm, even though she was burning up. Natalie slid her hands up Sarah's thighs and pulled her closer to her core. They both moaned at the intimacy of their embrace. Sarah moved her hips back and forth to get friction while she deepened the kiss. She was so brazen with Natalie. They were alone, under the stars, and Sarah couldn't think of anything else. When Natalie cupped her ass and held her against her lap, Sarah unbuttoned her pants. As much as she wanted to go inside and sprawl on the bed, there was something so decadent about taking charge and being outside with a fire raging behind them. Sarah pulled away to kick off her boots and peel off her pants, then returned to Natalie's lap.

"You are so beautiful," Natalie said.

Sarah pulled the blanket back up over her shoulders. The

chill nipped at her bare skin, but it was Natalie's touch that gave her chill bumps that raced over her entire body.

"Oh, you're cold. We can go inside."

"I'm not. Your touch is what's driving me crazy." Sarah's confession gave her confidence. She placed a tiny kiss on Natalie's neck and ran her tongue over her jaw on a path to Natalie's lips. She heard Natalie moan when she skipped over her mouth and made a path of tiny kisses on her other cheek and down to the other side of her neck. When she scraped her teeth across the soft skin and bit softly, she felt Natalie enter her. She hadn't realized that she was up on her knees waiting to be fucked. She didn't even feel Natalie's fingers slip under her panties. "Oh, God, yes."

She clutched Natalie's shoulders and stared into her eyes. She tried to keep eye contact, tried to have that extra connection, but it felt so good that her eyes fluttered shut. She rolled her head back and moved her hips against Natalie's hand slowly at first. When she picked up speed and the blanket fell to her waist, she didn't care. She slashed her mouth against Natalie's in a hard, deep kiss. She whimpered when Natalie varied the speed of her fingers from slow to fast and deep. She lost her breath when Natalie slid a third finger in and put her other hand at the back of her neck, holding her in place.

"I want to watch you come," Natalie said.

What she said wasn't romantic, but in that moment, it was the sexiest thing Sarah had ever heard. She stared into Natalie's eyes and moved her hips slowly, stretching with pleasure. She watched as Natalie opened her mouth and moaned whenever she did. It was as if Natalie was sharing the pleasure she felt.

"This feels so good, Nat," Sarah whispered against Natalie's mouth.

"You feel so good. So wet and tight."

Sarah didn't normally like to talk during sex, but Natalie's words excited her. Listening to her voice, the huskiness of it, built pressure inside her. She tilted her head back as Natalie increased speed, and just when she thought she couldn't take any more, when her body shook from being tense with want and need, she came hard. The orgasm rumbled out of her like thunder as intense pleasure washed over every part of her. She bit her lip to keep from crying out, but it was futile. She grabbed Natalie's shoulders and rode the orgasm until she was panting. When her hips stopped moving and her breath returned to normal, she put her forehead against Natalie's.

"That was truly amazing." She heard the shakiness of her voice and placed a small kiss on Natalie's mouth. She moaned again when Natalie gently slipped out of her. "I'm sorry if I hurt your hand."

"Are you kidding me? You and the way you came were the most beautiful things I've ever seen. My hand is fine."

Natalie's arms trembled as Sarah pulled the blanket back up over them. She ducked her head and rested it on Natalie's shoulder with a mixture of embarrassment and intensity. What had Natalie done to her? She had gone from reserved mother to wanton woman in the span of a week. Her legs were weak and her panties soaked, but she didn't want to leave the comfort and safety of Natalie's arms. This was not her. When was the last time she had an orgasm with that much intensity? The sting of tears pinched her eyes, and she begged herself not to cry. Not now.

"You have to be cold. Why don't we go inside?"

Sarah wanted to wait until she tamped down her emotions. Crying now would probably send the wrong message, or maybe the right one, and that scared her. "Two minutes." She hoped her voice was calm. Natalie rubbed her back softly until she stirred. "Okay. I'm ready." To her complete surprise, Natalie picked her up as though she weighed nothing and carried her up the stairs. Sarah put her hand on Natalie's chest. "What are you doing?"

"You don't have any shoes on, and the ground is cold." Without stopping to lock the door or even put out the fire, Natalie marched them straight back to her bedroom.

CHAPTER SEVENTEEN

Natalie's dream had come true. Half of her life she'd wanted Sarah, and now she was here, in her arms, in her bed. She wanted to do everything at once and also take her time. It was a tough spot to be in, but one she wouldn't trade for the world. She pulled back the covers and yanked off her own sweater and jeans before crawling in after Sarah.

"How are you so warm?" Sarah asked.

Natalie heard Sarah's teeth chatter as she adjusted to the coolness of the sheets. "Come here. I'm always warm, but my blood is boiling after what just happened." She pulled Sarah close and held her until she felt her relax. It was so hard to not tear off the rest of her clothes and taste her everywhere. Instead, Natalie started off slowly by kissing Sarah's neck. It was the right thing to do because Sarah's moans filled her ears and her hands roamed over Natalie, pulling her closer. She rolled Sarah onto her back and slipped between her legs. No, this wasn't going to work. She sat up and quickly peeled off Sarah's warm, wet panties before sinking back into her. "That's so much better."

"Not really." Sarah's whisper was low and quiet.

"Why not?" Natalie pulled up to look into Sarah's eyes.

"You're still dressed."

Natalie sat up, pulled her bra off, and moaned the second Sarah touched her breasts.

"You have the most beautiful breasts I've ever seen. So full and perfect."

Natalie hated them most days because her uniforms always had to be altered. But tonight, she was thankful. She allowed the pleasure for several seconds before pulling away to remove her panties as well. "Is this better?"

Natalie sank back down between Sarah's legs. She hooked the back of Sarah's knees over her elbows and pushed forward. They both moaned when their cores touched. Natalie had to be careful not to push too hard, or else she would come on the spot. She was so swollen and wet, and feeling the soft skin of Sarah's waxed pussy against her own almost set her over the edge.

"That feels so good," Sarah whispered.

Natalie kissed her hard and rocked against Sarah. It wasn't enough though. She needed to be inside her, feel her warmth and taste her essence. She didn't want to break apart their kiss, but loving every part of her was the most important thing right now. She sucked Sarah's neck and nibbled and bit at her skin all the way down to her breasts, pulling one nipple into her mouth, lavishing it with her tongue before doing the same for the other one. Sarah writhed under her touch, raising her hips whenever a part of Natalie's body came into contact with her pussy. It was fantastic to be with somebody who wasn't afraid of her own body or to experience pleasure.

She wrapped an arm around each thigh and kissed the soft skin on either side of Sarah's slit. She held Sarah's hips in place. She ran her tongue quickly across her swollen clit and made a path up and down, back and forth, tasting her, moaning with Sarah. When she locked her mouth on Sarah's clit and sucked, she slipped one, then two fingers inside her.

She fucked her and tasted her at the same time. Sarah was so wet that Natalie was able to find the perfect rhythm and depth. Her thrusts matched Sarah's hips. Within minutes Sarah came hard. She was even louder in the bedroom than she'd been outside. Natalie felt her passionate cries with every ounce of her body. She almost came at just how sexy and satisfied Sarah sounded.

"Fuck," Natalie whispered. She placed a tiny kiss on Sarah's clit before slipping out of her and crawling back up to kiss her. Sarah was still experiencing aftershocks, so Natalie thrust her hips against Sarah's. They were both surprised when she came again. "Fuck," Natalie said again. She wasn't much on cussing, but this whole experience brought out an animalistic side she didn't recognize. Sarah was perfect. Natalie rolled over and pulled Sarah into her arms. "I have no words."

"I have a ton of words, but none that I can form into coherent sentences," Sarah said.

Natalie knew she would never be the same. Tonight was life-changing. She had experienced several of those moments during her lifetime, and tonight was one of the most positive ones. Her heart throbbed. The pounding actually hurt, and she took a deep breath to steady herself.

"Are you okay?" Sarah cupped Natalie's face and pulled her down for a kiss.

Natalie nodded. She didn't want to spew out her emotions. She was still trying to weed through them herself. Before, Sarah was just a crush. She was a girl who kissed her at a party like it wasn't a big deal. But it was a huge deal to Natalie. For seventeen years Sarah would pop up in her mind. Maybe over time she'd romanticized her and made her perfect, but right here, in her arms, she was perfect. There wasn't anything she didn't like about Sarah. The pressure in her chest was building. The deep breath didn't help. She rolled onto her back and closed her eyes. Don't cry. Don't you dare cry, she thought. She felt Sarah climb on her body and kiss her earlobe and run her tongue down her neck.

"Why are you so perfect?" Sarah asked.

She felt Sarah's fingertips flutter down her throat, outline her collarbone, and curve around her breast. A soft noise escaped her mouth that, thankfully, wasn't a sob. She kept her eyes closed and got lost in the feeling of Sarah's hands on her body. Nothing else mattered right now. Not the future, not the past. Just this moment with the woman she loved. That's why she'd been so emotional lately. Love had slipped inside her carefully guarded heart, not once, not twice, but three times and squeezed hard. All in the span of a few weeks. She hadn't realized how heavy it had weighed on her until this very moment. She put her hand on top of Sarah's and squeezed.

"I'm not, but thank you," Natalie said.

Sarah's lips made a trail from the underside of Natalie's breast to her navel. Natalie wrapped her hands in Sarah's hair and tried her best not to move her hips or guide Sarah's head down. She was giving her complete control. Natalie was ready to come but waited not so patiently. Whatever Sarah had in store for her, she was ready. So very ready. "I'm going to show you how perfect I think you are." Her tongue made the joyous journey to the juncture of Natalie's thighs. Natalie held her breath and waited.

When the warmth of Sarah's mouth encircled her clit, she let herself go. Several tears slipped from the corner of her eyes, and she spread her legs farther apart to accommodate Sarah better. She was burning up and dying to come, but Sarah's mouth, hands, and warm body felt incredible. She wanted this feeling to last forever. She couldn't tell if thirty minutes passed or only thirty seconds. She raised her hips, trying to find the friction she needed to come, but Sarah held her down and continued licking and sucking until she had no choice but to explode. Natalie grabbed a pillow and yelled into it. She jerked with every wave that washed over her.

"What are you doing to that pillow?"

Natalie's laughter shook her entire body as she climbed down from an orgasm that left her breathless. "I have no idea. I just needed to hold something."

Sarah moved up Natalie to kiss her on her mouth, but left two fingers inside her. "Feeling you and hearing you come was amazing, Nat."

"I don't think I'm done," she said, smiling when she saw Sarah realize what she'd said. Sarah increased her speed. Natalie twisted so she was on her side facing Sarah. Their height difference was somewhat challenging, but by bending her knee, the new position gave Sarah complete access.

"I want to watch your face when you come," Sarah said.

Natalie kissed her deeply, passionately. Tasting herself on Sarah's lips was a natural aphrodisiac. She ended the kiss because she knew she was close again. Staring into Sarah's eyes, her mouth partially open, she waited for the build-up and tensed her muscles at the right time. Another orgasm rippled through her, and she tried hard to keep eye contact with Sarah but couldn't. She lowered her head and moved her hips against Sarah's hand and moaned and gasped with every thrust. "Fuck." When she slowed her hips, Sarah gently pulled out.

"You're beautiful and perfect. Watching you was the best thing I've ever done." Sarah brought Natalie's lips to her own and kissed her slowly, with even more emotion in this kiss. A shift took place between them. Something slipped out of place or snapped back in, Natalie couldn't tell which, but everything was clear. She had loved Sarah in high school and loved the woman in front of her. She was almost certain Sarah felt the same. "Nat, why are you crying?"

Fuck. Again with the tears. When did she get so soft? She quickly wiped them away and attempted to laugh them off, but the noise she made sounded more like a pained yelp. "Nothing. No reason."

"Come on, baby. Talk to me." Sarah ran her fingers over Natalie's neck and face, which only prompted fresh tears.

Natalie stopped Sarah's hand and brought her fingers up to her lips. She kissed them gently and entwined their fingers. "I just have a lot of emotions. So much is happening inside my heart, and I'm trying to process it."

Sarah took Natalie's hand and put it on her heart. "I know what you mean. Maybe this isn't the time, or maybe it's the perfect time, but I love you."

Natalie froze. Her rapid heartbeat echoed inside her, pounding faster and faster at what she heard. Maybe Sarah hadn't really said those words. Maybe Natalie wanted to hear them so badly, she only thought Sarah had said them. She opened her mouth and promptly closed it. "What?" She had to know for sure. She was afraid she would pass out from lack of oxygen. She relaxed and took a breath.

Sarah ran her fingers over Natalie's mouth and leaned up to place a kiss on her swollen lips. "I love you. I love you, Natalie Renee Strand. I was too young when we first kissed to understand what I was feeling, but right here, right now, I know without a doubt that it's love."

Natalie bowed her head so Sarah couldn't see her tears again, but it was useless. She put her head on Sarah's shoulder and cried. Her tears were for Sarah, for Harley, for Henry, for her father, for all the good in her life and all the bad that had led up to this moment. They were for her younger self who had sat on Ellie Shepherd's fireplace and kissed the most popular girl in school and never understood how it would affect her whole life. She took a deep breath, sniffled, and lifted her head to look at Sarah. "I can't tell you how long I've wanted to hear those words from you." She kissed Sarah fiercely, afraid to move her mouth and give her the opportunity to change her mind or not mean it. "I love you, too."

❖

Natalie stirred and, for a moment, she thought the body next to her was Henry. Then the previous evening flashed in her mind of Sarah's warm, supple body touching her everywhere, and she realized the woman of her dreams was still in bed with her. She pulled Sarah closer. "Why are you so far away from me?"

"Mmm. Good morning." Sarah placed a warm kiss on Natalie's cheek. "What time is it?"

"Not wow, what a fantastic, life-changing evening, but what time is it?" Natalie joked and kissed Sarah's forehead. "Good morning."

"Definitely life-changing. It's not every day I tell a beautiful woman that I love her. Or have really good sex. No, life-changing sex," Sarah said.

Natalie smiled. "Can I make you breakfast? Do we have time?"

Sarah looked at her phone and nodded. "I'm sure Harley was up late, so I probably have another hour. What do you want to do?"

Natalie slid out of bed and reached for Sarah.

"It's too cold outside the covers. Why can't we just stay in bed?"

"Okay. You stay here, and I'll be back with coffee."

Natalie kissed Sarah quickly and stepped into the bathroom. The hot water was exactly what her sore body needed. When was the last time she'd twisted like that or strained her muscles in such a delicious way?

"Make room for me."

Natalie smiled when she heard Sarah's voice and felt her fingertips slide down her back. She'd hoped Sarah would join her. She switched places with Sarah and put her under the water while she lathered the loofah. She took her time washing Sarah, giving extra attention to all her favorite places. They took turns washing, kissing, and laughing until the water grew lukewarm and they were forced to leave. "Let me grab you something warm to wear." She wrapped Sarah in an oversized towel and came back with a fluffy, pink robe that her parents had bought her years ago. Pink wasn't her color, so it hung in the closet, but it looked perfect on Sarah. Natalie slipped on sweatpants and a T-shirt and started coffee. "We still have banana-nut bread, pumpkin bread, or I can make us omelets or pancakes or both."

"I'm going to need a lot of protein to keep up with you," Sarah said.

It wasn't a one-time thing. Deep down, Natalie knew that, but hearing the words from Sarah made her heart swell. "Then how about a high-protein scramble? Do we have time?" She felt Sarah's hands cover her own.

"Nat, don't worry about the time. Everyone's fine. Nobody called. I can go home when I want. Let's have a nice breakfast, and then we can go see our babies, okay?"

Natalie took a deep breath. She'd never dated a single mother before. She didn't know the protocol for sleepovers. Did Sarah have to sneak in? Or would she walk in the door as if she was gone overnight all of the time? "Okay. Is there anything you don't eat in omelets?"

"Onions and tomatoes. Everything else is fine," Sarah said.

Natalie poured them a cup of coffee and started breakfast. She was a little nervous with Sarah watching her. They talked about foods they liked, foods they didn't. Natalie didn't like cilantro, but Sarah loved it and put it in everything. Natalie loved sweets, but Sarah wasn't a fan. "It's like we have nothing in common." Natalie held her hands up as if surrendering. "We might as well just stop now."

Sarah walked over to her and kissed her soundly. "I'm not walking away this time, Sheriff. I'll leave out the cilantro and eat more cake. Deal?"

Natalie bowed her head for another kiss. "Sounds perfect." She served them breakfast and sat beside Sarah instead of across from her. She wanted to stay close for as long as she could. Even though Sarah told her time wasn't an issue, she felt it burning in the pit of her stomach. It was hard not to keep looking at the time. She loved it when Sarah put her hand on Natalie's knee and squeezed it for no other reason than to have a connection. Sarah knew how to show love, and Natalie melted every time. A touch, a kiss, a kind gesture.

"I guess I should get dressed. I don't want to leave this fairy tale though." Sarah wrapped her arms around Natalie's waist and put her head on her shoulder.

It was the best feeling. All the walls between them were down. Natalie held Sarah, and they stood there in her kitchen with their arms around one another. She had never been so sure of anything in her life. A peace washed over her when she realized that Sarah wasn't leaving, that this wasn't the end. This was only the beginning. Not again, Natalie thought. Tears swelled behind her eyelids, but this time she was able to blink them away. "I understand. We will have plenty of overnights, plenty of showers, plenty of time." Natalie watched as Sarah got dressed. She was beautiful and all hers. She smiled when Sarah straddled her lap and stroked the back of her neck.

"Thank you for last night."

Natalie raised her eyebrow and kissed Sarah. "It meant the world to me. You know that, right?"

Sarah nodded. "I'm sorry, Nat."

"Shh. There's nothing to be sorry for. We had to live the lives we did to reach this point." She kissed Sarah's hand. "This is just the beginning."

"I love you."

"I love you, too."

CHAPTER EIGHTEEN

When are Sheriff Natalie and Henry getting here?"
Sarah smiled at Harley's impatience. Her daughter
was on the back of the couch with her nose pressed against the
window, waiting for Natalie's Jeep to pull into the driveway.
She, too, was anxious to see Natalie again, even though she'd
just seen her early that morning. When the alarm had beeped at
five, they'd both groaned at the invasion, but Sarah had slipped
out of Natalie's bed, thrown on her clothes, and sneaked back
home before Harley woke. Aunt Judy had busted her but
hadn't said anything. Only held up her hand for a high five on
her way downstairs.

"I hope it doesn't start snowing," Aunt Judy said. She and
Sarah set the table after Uncle Bob added the leaf extension to
the dining-room table. Sarah added a cornucopia centerpiece
that Harley had made in school out of construction paper and
foam. It smelled like Elmer's glue and Crayola crayons and
resembled a football more than a horn, but it was precious, and
her little girl had made it.

"I'm not super thrilled with cold weather, but it's a nice
change of pace after being in Texas for so long," Sarah said.
She put her arm around her aunt, and they watched as Harley
drew on the condensation on the window. "I'll wash the
window after she's done."

"Don't worry about it. Maybe one day she'll be an artist."

Sarah studied the artwork closer and looked back at the centerpiece. "No. Nope. I don't think that's going to be her calling."

Aunt Judy laughed. "Probably Supreme Court justice. She's very calm and very smart. Not overly emotional and not overly artistic."

"Mom, when are they getting here?"

"Soon. In one minute. Count down from sixty," Sarah said. While Harley counted, Sarah checked on the turkey. After sleeping until seven, Sarah had gotten up to start cooking with Aunt Judy. The turkey was all her responsibility. Aunt Judy had made mashed potatoes, stuffing with cranberries, and green-bean casserole. Natalie was bringing rolls and candied yams, and Linda was responsible for the pies.

"I really like Linda. It's nice to have a new friend. I mean, I've always known her, but because of you girls, we're friends. And we have a lot in common. With Bob at the lodge a lot, it's nice to call her up and make plans."

"I'm happy you're friends, too."

"They're here! They're here!" Harley jumped off the couch and ran to the door.

"Harley Nicole! Put your boots on before you go outside." Sarah's message registered at the last second. Harley slipped on her boots and ran out to greet Henry. She threw her arms around his neck and kissed his nose.

"You just saw him yesterday," Sarah said. She slipped on her boots and jacket to help Linda and Natalie bring food inside.

"You know there are only six of us eating. Five and a half, really." Sarah kissed Natalie and grabbed two bags from the back of the Jeep.

"Hi, babe. Yeah. Tell that to my mom. Most of these are hers."

"Mmm. I've missed your mouth."

Natalie kissed her again. "I've missed everything about you."

"You win. Come on. Let's get inside before they send out a search party."

"Too late. We're here," Aunt Judy said. They turned and found Uncle Bob's outstretched arms ready to carry in the bulk of Linda's baking. He made a production of staggering under the weight of the three containers Natalie handed him.

"Thank you for having us over for Thanksgiving," Natalie said.

"Thanksgiving is for family and friends, and we're so thankful to have all three of you in our lives," Sarah said. She took Natalie and Linda's coats and hung them in the closet. "Have a seat. Dinner's in half an hour. We have cheese and crackers, if anyone can't wait that long."

Natalie headed straight for the tray. "Since my only contribution was rolls and yams, I didn't eat a lot. Usually I graze while Mom and I are cooking." She grabbed two crackers and two pieces of cheese and sat on the couch next to Sarah.

"How's your day so far?" The cute flush that peeked up from Natalie's collar made Sarah's pulse quicken.

"It's a fantastic Thanksgiving. Best one so far." Natalie winked at her.

"I agree. New friends, old family, new beginnings, old comforts," Sarah said.

Natalie leaned closer to Sarah. "Old comforts? Tell me you don't mean me." She put her hand on her heart.

Sarah tapped Natalie's hand. "You are part of my new everything. New friends, new beginnings."

"We'll talk about the friends thing later." Natalie playfully growled at her.

Uncle Bob, a diehard football fan, who not only had the NFL channel, but recorded all the highlights on ESPN, had *The Little Mermaid* on for Harley. When Sarah asked him about it, he said, "Nobody cares about the Lions anyway. Football is all about the Seahawks."

When Sarah's parents FaceTimed to wish everyone a happy Thanksgiving, Aunt Judy waved to her sister and brother-in-law and excused herself to check on the food. The call ended right as Aunt Judy finished the gravy.

"Let's eat. Please, everyone, take a seat. Sarah and I will bring the food out," Aunt Judy said.

"How come there are seven plates, Aunt Judy?" Sarah asked.

"There are seven of us."

Sarah did a quick head count. "I count six."

"You're right. I count seven," Harley said. She reached out to stroke Henry's soft fur.

Sarah mouthed thank you to her aunt and guided Harley to the dining room table. "Henry can sit next to you, but he eats on the floor. It's just easier for him down there."

"Can I eat on the floor with him?"

"No, honey. We want to see your adorable face at the table, not under it," Sarah said.

Aunt Judy poured five glasses of wine and passed them around the table. Uncle Bob poured a glass of apple cider in a wineglass for Harley and told her to use both of her hands. Sarah looked the other way as Harley balanced the drink.

"A toast." Uncle Bob stood to get everyone's attention. "This year we have so much to be thankful for. So much I don't know where to begin. I'm going to try hard not to cry, but if I do, just pretend I'm not."

Sarah winked at her uncle and hardened herself against his upcoming words. He wasn't a man of many, but he lived his life with his heart on his sleeve.

"We have our health and one another. This year, our lovely niece and her beautiful daughter came here to start a new beginning in Spruce Mountain. Having both of you around has been a blessing. Thank you for enriching our lives." He tilted his glass and took a sip. Everyone else did the same. "We are thankful Linda and Natalie are in our lives, too. Your friendship is appreciated. We're thankful Natalie is the sheriff of our small town and for all the good she has done. She was the driving force behind finding Harley, and she's the reason our niece wakes up with a smile on her face and a skip in her step."

Sarah blushed at the sudden attention, her cheeks warming under Natalie's gaze. Just this morning, she was under Natalie, her legs spread, clutching the headboard as Natalie fucked her hard. Her cheeks warmed even more at the memory, and she shook her head briefly to get the thought out of her head. She focused her attention back on Uncle Bob.

"And a special toast to Henry. Without him...Well, I don't even want to think about where we would be without him."

Both Harley and Natalie reached down to pet him. He wagged his tail and licked both their hands.

"Henry is the real hero. He left the house because he knew something was wrong. He found Harley and stayed with her, protecting her overnight. And he found me and made sure I followed him to find her," Natalie said.

Sarah stood. "It's my turn. I am thankful for my beautiful daughter, Harley. She has given me joy and laughter and has been the best thing that has ever happened to me." Sarah kissed the top of Harley's head. "And thank you, Aunt Judy and Uncle Bob, for allowing us into your home. I appreciate the fresh start, and I love you both dearly. Thank you, Linda, for working with Aunt Judy to encourage Natalie and me to share space. I've had an amazing time reconnecting with you, Natalie. Thank you for giving me a second chance." Sarah paused while glasses were clinked. When she had everyone's attention, she continued. "And thank you, Henry, for taking care of my baby, my heart, and bringing her back to me safely."

Henry wagged his tail and barked at the sudden attention. Harley tried to give him a drink of her cider, but Sarah quickly grabbed the glass so it didn't break or spill. "Let's get Henry his own drink."

Aunt Judy quickly returned with a bowl of water and put it on the floor in front of him. "Okay. How about we say the dinner prayer and eat all this food?" They held hands while Bob said their family Thanksgiving prayer.

Sarah looked around the table at all the happy faces. She really did have so much to be thankful for. She had her daughter back after the worst fear a parent could ever experience. She had a fresh start on life, a new girlfriend, and a career that was just beginning. Her heart was full.

❖

"I'm going to drive Mom home, and then I'll come back, okay?" Natalie kissed Sarah's temple.

"Natalie, don't leave yet," Harley said. She was on the floor in front of the television curled up with Henry.

"Baby, I'm just going to run my mom home, but I'll be back. Will you watch Henry for me?"

Sarah melted at how wonderful Natalie was with her daughter. Not everyone wanted an instant family. Dating a single mom wasn't for everyone, but Natalie jumped right in without overstepping. She'd never thought she would find somebody so quickly because she wasn't looking.

"I'll be back in ten minutes." Natalie kissed her and left with Linda.

"She's pretty wonderful, you know?" Aunt Judy handed her a cup of cider when the door closed.

"I'm lucky, without a doubt," Sarah said.

"I couldn't be happier."

"Mom, how late can I stay up tonight?" Harley asked.

It was already after eight, and Sarah knew she wanted to see Natalie before she went to bed. "Nine, but no arguing then, okay?" She watched Harley high-five Uncle Bob and drop back into her spot next to Henry. To kill time before Natalie returned, Sarah finished wiping down the kitchen. She finished her cider and rinsed out the cup right as Natalie returned, ten minutes later, as promised. Harley jumped up to greet her and hugged her like she'd been gone for hours. She pulled Natalie over to the couch and sat next to her, her tiny body brimming with energy.

"Sit here with us, Mommy."

Sarah sat on the other side of Harley and held her hand. Warmth spread from within at the look Natalie gave her. It was a look of love, and she welcomed it. She hadn't felt this way ever. For the first time, this was a real family. Her real family. Natalie, Harley, Uncle Bob, and Aunt Judy made her feel complete. As much as she had fought it in the beginning and thought Spruce Mountain was just a blip on the GPS, a tiny dot on the map where she would reset their lives and move on, looking around at these wonderful people, Sarah knew what Spruce Mountain really was to her. It was home.

EPILOGUE

D on't let Henry get too close. I don't want him stepping on
any nails."

Natalie looked at the new addition being built on her
house, on *their* house, and smiled. It was coming along nicely.
The original structure was twelve hundred square feet, but they
were adding an additional six hundred so that Harley could
have a bigger bedroom and Sarah would have a large office
with a separate entrance for her customers. Her client list was
growing, but true to her word, she kept her job at the library so
she could take Harley to and from school.

"I won't let him. He's being good," Harley said.

Henry looked up at her and woofed. Natalie trusted him
one hundred percent. He was where he wanted to be, where he
deserved to be, with the people he loved and who loved him
just as much.

"Are you being a good boy, Henry?"

Another woof and a tail wag. Natalie certainly didn't
want another trip to the vet for a nail or splinter in his paw.
Their last visit had been awkward enough, with her present
girlfriend and her ex-girlfriend in the same room. The mood
was professional enough, and Sarah and Dr. Wallace seemed to
communicate just fine, but Natalie's anxiety level was through
the roof.

"Natalie, when will they have the walls up?" Harley asked.

"By this weekend. When we get back from our trip, we can pick out paint colors. Have you decided what color you want?"

Harley put her finger on her lips and looked up and away, as if contemplating a life-changing decision. If paint was the hardest decision she would have to make, then she and Sarah were doing something right. "I like pink. Or maybe purple. Can I have both?"

"I don't see why not." Natalie looked at her watch. "Are you ready for camp?"

"Aw, Natalie. Do I have to go?"

It broke her heart to not give Harley everything she wanted, but she couldn't take her to work, and they had already signed her up for dance camp this week. Summer break had just started in Spruce Mountain, and Harley didn't want to attend summer school. They had worked out a morning schedule with Judy, Bob, and Linda, but getting through the first week was going to be hard. Harley didn't like ballet, but it was the only thing available. Sarah would pick her up after work every day, and then on Friday, they were off to spend a few days at Disneyland. "I know you don't want to, but at least by the end of the week, we'll have a lot of fun."

"I've been thinking. We should stay home so Henry won't be alone."

"Henry will be with Linda until Sunday, and then Aunt Judy will have him until Monday night, when we get home." They had originally planned to spend a full week at the theme park, but they'd had to cut it short because Harley refused to be away from Henry for more than four days. That was their compromise. Truth be told, Natalie didn't want to be gone for that long either, but she could tell Sarah needed to be around people. New people, not just the same ones who recycled through her day.

Harley walked through the unfinished part of the addition and reached for Natalie's hand. "Okay. But ballet is stupid. Can Henry go to camp with me?"

Natalie looked at Henry. "I don't think he wants to dance, but he would probably love to go in to work with me." When Sarah and Harley had first moved in, Henry would spend the mornings at the station. Natalie would drop him off at the house later in the afternoon so he would be at home when the girls arrived. "Deputy Dog has been missed."

Harley laughed with that sweet, innocent giggle that made Natalie melt. "Deputy Dog. That's funny."

"I won't make him wear his badge though. It's summer and it's too hot," Natalie said. Another laugh. "Let's go. Henry can ride in the back with you." She grabbed the tiny backpack full of whatever seven-year-olds needed and put it in the back seat with Harley. "You ready, big guy?" Henry kissed her hand. She stroked his muzzle before gently closing the door.

"Natalie, do we have time for ice cream?"

"I'm sorry, sweetie, but no. Plus, you don't want to dance with a belly full of ice cream, do you?"

"Yes."

Natalie smiled. This kid was something else. "We'll have some after dinner." Big sigh. She parked near the dance studio and rolled the windows down. After helping Harley out, she turned to Henry. "You're in charge." Tail wag.

"Are you sure we can't do something else?" Harley grabbed her hand and walked slowly toward the door, her backpack dragging on the sidewalk.

Natalie took the backpack and opened the door for Harley. "Look. Isn't that your friend Rory?"

"Rory! Hi!"

Harley let go of Natalie's hand and ran over to her friend. She smiled as they hugged and laughed. Suddenly ballet wasn't going to be as bad as they both thought. After watching the children play and realizing Harley was going to make it through the afternoon just fine, she waved bye to them and headed out to the car. According to her watch, she still had a few minutes left on her lunch hour. "Okay, Henry. Move over. We have time to go say hi to Sarah." She turned the car around and pointed it toward the library.

Mary Cooper always lit up when Natalie popped in. Natalie suspected she was a lesbian but was very quiet about it. If she had a lover, the town never knew. Faith made sure to keep the department informed of all the gossip. As much as Natalie rolled her eyes at it, secretly she appreciated it. Mary's name never came up.

"Hello, Sheriff. And Deputy Dog." Mary closed the book she was reading and gave Natalie her full attention.

"Hi, Mary. I'm looking for Sarah. Is she around? She forgot her purse this morning."

It had been a surprise to both of them when Natalie asked Sarah and Harley to move in, and an even bigger surprise when Sarah accepted. It was getting too hard to be apart every day and every night, and in a moment of frustration and extreme emotional stress, Natalie had asked Sarah and Harley to move in with her. It was three o'clock Christmas morning, and Sarah was putting on her boots to leave Natalie's to be home in time for Harley. Natalie had hated that she was missing Harley's big morning, with the magic of Christmas and Santa fading away the older she got. Sarah stood and faced Natalie.

"What did you just say?"
This was the first time they had produced heat between

them that wasn't passion. "I know it sounds crazy, but damn it, I love you. And I love Harley. Henry and I hate that you and I have to sneak around all the time. I hate that you are looking for a place to live when Henry and I know you belong here with us." She threw the covers back and stood, hands on her hips, ignoring that she was naked.

"First of all, did you just add Henry into the mix because he's adorable and you wanted to sweeten the deal?"

"Are you calling my wonderfully creative suggestion a 'deal'?" Natalie wasn't sure if she was angry or on the verge of laughing, standing there naked while Sarah was fully dressed. Everything hinged on the next few seconds—her happiness, her future, her heart. Why had she done it? Maybe Sarah didn't want to or maybe she wasn't ready. And, if she wasn't mistaken, the first night they all got together at Tanner's, Sarah had said she never wanted to marry again, not that Natalie was asking. And not that she wasn't thinking about it, because she would marry Sarah in a heartbeat.

Feeling vulnerable, Natalie slipped into the hideous pink robe Sarah had been wearing and started listing all the reasons why it was a great idea. "I hate saying good-bye at night. I hate missing out on all of Harley's big events. I hate it when you leave the bed at three in the morning like we're doing something wrong. Harley accepts me. She's seen us kiss and hold one another. Why can't we just all be together?"

"Nat, you know I just signed the paperwork to rent the Thompsons' house."

Natalie moved closer to Sarah. "So, that's not a no." She put her arm around Sarah's waist and, with her free hand, smoothed down the deep crease between her eyebrows that showed up whenever Sarah was deep in thought. "And you signed month-to-month. So, tomorrow we'll call Peggy and say thanks, but no thanks."

"And they're dropping off the Pod with all our stuff next week."

Natalie smoothed down another crease on Sarah's forehead with the pad of her thumb.

"We can reroute them to this address. The house is only five minutes away."

Sarah threw up her hands. "How is every single thing only five minutes away?"

Natalie shrugged. "Small-town life." She pulled Sarah closer and kissed her. "Baby, just say yes. Just move in here. It's going to work out. We're perfect together. All four of us." She held her breath when Sarah put her head on Natalie's shoulder. Natalie knew it was a lot for Sarah to think about.

"Everything is happening so fast. I just got here less than three months ago. What are people going to think?"

"They are going to think 'oh, what a perfect couple' and 'it's about time that sheriff found somebody perfect for her.' Nobody is going to say anything negative about you," Natalie said.

"What about Dr. Wallace?"

Natalie rolled her eyes. "I can't believe we're talking about her right now. Of all things."

"I can't believe you hate pink, because you look beautiful in it," Sarah said.

"Only eight-year-olds wear pink. But if you move in, I'll wear pink whenever you want."

"Well, how can I say no?"

Natalie squeezed Sarah until she grunted. "I love you so much."

"I love you, too."

Natalie smiled at the memory. That had been their only fight in six months. Their life together was too good to be true.

Harley had accepted her immediately, and they had slipped into their new lives as if they'd always been together as a family.

"Hi, babe. What are you doing here? Is Harley at ballet?" Sarah kissed Natalie first, then Henry.

"I had to drag her kicking and screaming. It was terrible." At Sarah's horrified look, Natalie assured her everything was fine, and Harley was perfectly happy since Rory was there. "The big guy and I had a few minutes, so I thought we'd stop by and just say hi and drop this off." Natalie slid Sarah's purse to her on the counter.

"Thank you. And? Did she try to talk you out of it?"

Natalie had heard their argument this morning before Sarah left for work. Harley never threw tantrums but had tried really hard to plead her case. Natalie would have caved and taken Harley to the station armed with iPad, Nintendo Switch, and coloring books. Instead, she'd wisely kept out of it, kissed them both quickly, and left earlier than she wanted. "She suggested ice cream, which I wavered on, but I decided to take her to camp since she was expected. With Rory there, I don't think there will be a problem getting her to dance any more this week."

"Thank God for best friends," Sarah said.

"It's only a matter of time before play dates start." Natalie was looking forward to having more kids at the house. Henry would love it. "Rory's a great kid. He can visit any time."

"Agreed. Now go do sheriff stuff, and I'm going to count the hours until I can go pick up the kiddo. No, I'm not stressing. Not at all."

Natalie kissed her again. "She's not going anywhere ever again. Not until college. Can we home-school college?"

"I don't think so. Let's get through the high school years first. We might want her to go far away for college," Sarah said.

Natalie's radio clicked to life. "Your new cadets are waiting at the station, Sheriff." Faith's loud message made them both smile.

"10-4. I'll be right there." She kissed Sarah, and she and Henry walked out of the library, but not before stopping for several patrons who wanted to pet him. He was the perfect ambassador and greeter for a sleepy town like Spruce Mountain. He was already a hero, so people went out of their way to say hello. He wasn't as skittish as he was when he first got to town. Natalie always smiled at how he lit up at the attention.

When Natalie arrived with lights on and a few short bursts of the siren, approximately fifteen kids standing in a line outside of the station cheered. She had to admit, it made her heart swell.

"Welcome to the sheriff's department," Natalie said. She shook Principal Mickey's hand and waved at the kids, who gleefully waved back. It melted Natalie's heart to see how excited they were to learn something new. She and Mickey had come up with an afternoon program at the station on Mondays for summer school kids to learn about law enforcement. Harley's suggestion last fall about kids climbing into the patrol car gave Natalie an idea. She came up with a four-week program where she, Joshua, and David would take five kids each and discuss the importance of whatever subject they specialized in and, every week, rotate. It was a good way to get the kids excited about officers and not fear them. The final Monday, before the July 4th weekend, they would all earn honorary deputy badges.

"Who wants to learn about being a deputy?" Natalie asked. Several hands were raised. She cheered with them and issued the badges inside.

Faith greeted them with cold lemonade and had them

sit in the conference room, where Natalie would kick off the program with a quick chat about what it was like for her as a sheriff of Spruce Mountain.

"I grew up in Spruce Mountain, and I know a lot of your parents. We went to school together. Principal Mickey and I knew each other pretty well." She left out the part about him being a bully and doing shitty things to her and half of their parents. "I went away to college to study the law and was a police officer in Denver, Colorado. Who knows where Denver is?" Several kids raised their hands. "I came back and was a deputy here like Deputy David and Deputy Joshua and worked my way up to be sheriff."

"What does a sheriff do?"

"I make sure people follow the laws, and if they don't, I remind them."

"Do you arrest a lot of people?"

"I don't. Most people in town follow the rules. If you follow the rules, you don't get into trouble. Like at school. You don't want to have to go see Principal Mickey if you are in trouble. He's like the sheriff at school."

Natalie spoke to them until they divided up into groups. Joshua explained the equipment each deputy wore. Then he explained how the sheriff's department was a safe space and they could always ask for help at the station or if they saw any of them out on patrol. David showed them the radios, the community website, and the cameras around town. Natalie had her group in the patrol cars and the sheriff's van. Their department wasn't big, but they provided a lot of good information, and getting the kids on the right side of the law early was a great idea. She knew the power she wielded just because she made it a point to know most of the people in town. People were less likely to act up if they had a personal connection with an officer.

After the kids left, the four of them fell into chairs, exhausted.

"I don't know how teachers do it," Faith said. She put her head on her desk. "Even though this is a great idea, I feel beat up."

Natalie took off her hat and ran her fingers through her hair. "We'll get through this. I think it went well, but yeah. I could use a nap."

Both David and Joshua were pumped. Not that Natalie didn't enjoy her job, but now that she had a family, she was more excited to be done with the day and get home to them. Since she was going to be gone next Monday, Betty was planning to fill in. Natalie never took time off. She always felt guilty or that something bad would happen if she was gone. Disneyland was a big step for her. Four days off was a long time.

When it was time to go home, she and Henry climbed into the patrol car. "You were such a good boy with the kids. I hope you're okay with it." Henry wagged his tail. She knew he probably didn't understand her, but her tone was gentle, and he always responded sweetly when she spoke softly. It was amazing how much love she'd found in less than a year. First Sarah, then Harley, then Henry. Even her mother was livelier and more involved in her life now that Natalie had a family.

Seventeen years ago, the most popular girl in high school had kissed her. And it wasn't a dare or a bet. It was something she wanted to do. And Natalie was surprised at how quickly she'd accepted Sarah's kiss. She hadn't hesitated at all. Instinct had kicked in, and she'd kissed her back as though it was something they did all the time.

When Sarah had slipped quietly back into town, Natalie had known they were meant to be together. Life and love were richer with Sarah and Harley. Everything had meaning, and the world was more colorful. Seeing life through the eyes of a seven-year-old was precious, and Natalie felt blessed to be a part of their lives. And the big furry guy next to her? She had so much love for him, she thought her heart would burst. She gave his head a pat and shook his paw when he offered it. "I'm ready to see the girls. How about you?" She laughed when he licked her cheek. "You are, too. Okay, Henry. Let's go home."

HENRY

Something exploded inside Ellen Connors and woke her from her midafternoon nap. She had drifted off sometime after eating a small lunch and drinking her cup of tea. The pressure in her chest made her sit up sharply, and she dropped to her knees. She hadn't fallen far, but the tumble shocked her joints, and her hip, recently replaced, burned like fire. She hissed and expelled the air from her lungs and breathed in short little bursts as if she were in labor. The pain was worse than she ever imagined. Damn it, she wasn't ready to go. Not like this. She had to reach the barn before she left this world.

Determination kept her damaged heart pumping. She pulled herself up but remained bent over, with her fist at her chest as if the pressure of her hand would relieve some of the ache. She couldn't find the key to the barn, but she would figure out a way to get inside once she made it to the door. *If* she made it, she prayed. The throbbing in her chest had subsided, or she had pushed through the sharpness of it. It was as if her body knew she still had one final thing to do. Thankfully, the door was unlocked, and she was able to grasp the handle and push her frail body through it. The golden retriever tied up in the barn looked slightly malnourished and eyed her warily.

"My sweet, sweet boy. Are you okay?" She hadn't seen

her dog for months, and tears sprang to her eyes when she saw what her son had done to her one true love left in this world. She slowly slid down the stall wall and pled for the dog to come to her. He paced back and forth and eventually slowed when he recognized she wasn't going to hurt him. She held out a cookie that she had stashed in the pocket of her cardigan. He snatched it from her and crunched hungrily. Ellen dug around in her pockets for anything else for him to eat but came up empty. "Come here, Henry."

She'd named him after her late husband, William Henry Connors, and he had been her companion for almost four years. When her son had moved back to the area to take care of her after she fell and broke her hip three months ago, he'd put Henry in the barn. He'd promised to take care of him, and after she healed, the dog would be welcomed back in the house. Even though she begged to see him while she recovered, her son always made excuses. Anger had fueled the last few minutes of her life.

"I won't have you living like this." She clenched her teeth, scooted to the stake that held him a prisoner, and worked hard on the rope around his neck. She accepted his gentle kisses while she struggled to loosen the tight knot. Once he was free, she lay on the straw and looked at him. "I'm so sorry, Henry. Please forgive me. I didn't know you weren't being cared for. Go now. Before he returns. Go find a better home."

She pressed her fist to her chest again and watched as he struggled between staying and leaving. She shooed him away when they heard a car door slam, and once he escaped, she closed her eyes. Her son was an asshole. How did two nice people like herself and Will raise such a spoiled, heartless, selfish man? Well, the joke was on him. She'd left everything, including the money in the two bank accounts, the house, and the land, to the Oregon Humane Society. She had ensured that the will was iron-clad, and after she'd seen how Henry was treated, the pinch of guilt in her heart that she hadn't left anything to her only child was erased. She no longer cared that her son got nothing. She relaxed and closed her eyes for the last time. The final prayer that left her heart was that Henry find a family who would love him as much as she did.

❖

Henry learned the hard way to trust no one. He knew his owner wanted him to leave the bad place, so he ran. He wandered through fields and thick woods, not knowing where to go. He never stopped unless he was exhausted. Food came in the form of anything he could find in trash cans, dumpsters, and bags tossed out of windows near the highway. Sometimes begging worked at rest stops and gas stations. Most people assumed he belonged to somebody. Children were good at giving him food. He wouldn't take it from their hands but would wait until they dropped it on the ground or threw it his way. He had a better chance of finding food and remaining inconspicuous in smaller towns. People didn't question a loose dog as much as they did in the big cities.

Once, he found a solitary bag outside a grocery store with a whole chicken that he managed to dig out before somebody chased him away. He liked this town. Cars drove slower, and people talked to one another. And the stores smelled wonderful. They reminded him of his old home, when his owner baked cookies and cakes and gave him samples and asked him what he thought. He always approved. This store smelled familiar. Maybe somebody here would take him home. He was so happy at the thought that when the woman with the big hat approached him, he let her pet him. She was nice and didn't seem threatening at all. Maybe she was his new person.

❖

Guns scared him. Their loud booming sound made him cower in fear. When the man shot at him, he almost left the town for good. He stopped running when he heard her voice. She was angry at the man with the gun. He almost went to her when she called out for him, but he was frightened. He didn't want her to get hurt, so he ran. It took days, but he finally found her house in the small town. He knew she lived there because her scent was everywhere. The house was dark though. He would have to wait until morning to see her again. He squeezed through a loose board in the shed at the end of the driveway, found a blanket in the corner of the dry place, and curled up to sleep. He felt safe for the first time. He was hungry, but now that he had found his person, he knew she would take care of him.

She cooked for him, like his old owner had. And when he sneaked onto her bed to protect her at night, she didn't make him get down. She snuggled with him instead. The bath wasn't great, but he liked smelling better than dirt and garbage. He sat like a good boy when she brushed him. She was so gentle with him and made sure all his tangles were gone. She made sure he always had food and fresh water. She was reserved with him, though, and he desperately wanted her to love him. Maybe over time he would show her that he wasn't going to run away. Not anymore.

When the little girl went missing, he knew he had to do something. He saw how his new person was upset and distraught. He would help. He knew the woods well after spending weeks in them. There were plenty of places for the little girl to hide, especially if she was scared like he was. His person called out for him, but he kept running, determined to help. When he found the little girl, it was dark, and she was crying. He smelled fear on her and approached her cautiously. He wagged his tail and crawled to her, showing her his belly. He meant no harm. He wanted to protect her until his person showed up. When the little girl put her arms around his neck and cried, he vowed to get her home safely. They fell asleep inside a hollowed tree trunk, and he kept her warm. In the morning he would find his person and get her to safety.

The birds were singing, so he knew it was going to be light soon. The little girl was sleeping hard, so now was the time to find help. He sneaked away and ran fast through the forest. He knew where his person lived and was going to run straight for her house. When he heard her calling out for the little girl, he barked. She was here, just like he hoped she would be. He barked again. She yelled for him. He raced to her and barked, saying he knew where the little girl was and that she needed to follow him. Once he'd led her to the little girl, he lay down and watched as his person and the little girl cried. He knew he'd done a good thing. He was never going to leave them again.

When the little girl and her mother moved in with them, he was so happy. He was living his best life. He was always with somebody and never alone or tied up. Most of the time, he was with his person, but sometimes he would walk the little girl to school and stay at the library with her mom. He loved his new life. He had found three people who loved him, a town who accepted him, especially when he rode in the important car with the red and blue lights, and most importantly, a loving place he could again call home.

About the Author

Multi-award-winning author Kris Bryant was born in Tacoma, Washington, but has lived all over the world and now considers Kansas City her home. She received her BA in English from the University of Missouri and spends a lot of her time buried in books. She enjoys hiking, photography, spending time with her family, and her dog, Molly (who gets more attention than she does on Facebook).

Her first novel, *Jolt*, was a Lambda Literary Finalist and Rainbow Awards Honorable Mention. Her second book, *Whirlwind Romance*, was a Rainbow Runner-up for Contemporary Romance. *Taste* was a Rainbow Awards Honorable Mention for Contemporary Romance. *Forget Me Not* was selected by the American Library Association's 2018 Over the Rainbow book list and was a Golden Crown finalist for Contemporary Romance. *Breakthrough* won a 2019 Goldie for Contemporary Romance. *Listen* was an Ann Bannon Popular Choice finalist and Golden Crown winner. Kris can be reached at krisbryantbooks@gmail or www.krisbryant.net, @krisbryant14.

Books Available From Bold Strokes Books

Best Practice by Carsen Taite. When attorney Grace Maldonado agrees to mentor her best friend's little sister, she's prepared to confront Perry's rebellious nature, but she isn't prepared to fall in love. Legal Affairs: one law firm, three best friends, three chances to fall in love. (978-1-63555-361-1)

Home by Kris Bryant. Natalie and Sarah discover that anything is possible when love takes the long way home. (978-1-63555-853-1)

Keeper by Sydney Quinne. With a new charge under her reluctant wing—feisty, highly intelligent math wizard Isabelle Templeton—Keeper Andy Bouchard has to prevent a murder or die trying. (978-1-63555-852-4)

One More Chance by Ali Vali. Harry Bastantes planned a future with Desi Thompson until the day Desi disappeared without a word, only to walk back into her life sixteen years later. (978-1-63555-536-3)

Renegade's War by Gun Brooke. Freedom fighter Aurelia DeCallum regrets saving the woman called Blue. She fears it will jeopardize her mission, and secretly, Blue might end up breaking Aurelia's heart. (978-1-63555-484-7)

The Other Women by Erin Zak. What happens in Vegas should stay in Vegas, but what do you do when the love you find in Vegas changes your life forever? (978-1-63555-741-1)

The Sea Within by Missouri Vaun. Time is running out for Dr. Elle Graham to convince Captain Jackson Drake that the only thing that can save future Earth resides in the past, and rescue her broken heart in the process. (978-1-63555-568-4)

To Sleep With Reindeer Justine Saracen. In Norway under Nazi occupation, Marrit, an Indigenous woman, and Kirsten, a Norwegian resister, join forces to stop the development of an atomic weapon. (978-1-63555-735-0)

Twice Shy by Aurora Rey. Having an ex with benefits isn't all it's cracked up to be. Will Amanda Russo learn that lesson in time to take a chance on love with Quinn Sullivan? (978-1-63555-737-4)

Z-Town by Eden Darry. Forced to work together to stay alive, Meg and Lane must find the centuries-old treasure before the zombies find them first. (978-1-63555-743-5)

Bet Against Me by Fiona Riley. In the high-stakes luxury real estate market, everything has a price, and as rival Realtors Trina Lee and Kendall Yates find out, that means their hearts and souls, too. (978-1-63555-729-9)

Broken Reign by Sam Ledel. Together on an epic journey in search of a mysterious cure, a princess and a village outcast must overcome life-threatening challenges and their own prejudice if they want to survive. (978-1-63555-739-8)

Just One Taste by CJ Birch. For Lauren, it only took one taste to start trusting in love again. (978-1-63555-772-5)

Lady of Stone by Barbara Ann Wright. Sparks fly as a magical emergency forces a noble embarrassed by her ability to submit to a low-born teacher who resents everything about her. (978-1-63555-607-0)

Last Resort by Angie Williams. Katie and Rhys are about to find out what happens when you meet the girl of your dreams but you aren't looking for a happily ever after. (978-1-63555-774-9)

Longing for You by Jenny Frame. When Debrek housekeeper Katie Brekman is attacked amid a burgeoning vampire-witch war, Alexis Villiers must go against everything her clan believes in to save her. (978-1-63555-658-2)

Money Creek by Anne Laughlin. Clare Lehane is a troubled lawyer from Chicago who tries to make her way in a rural town full of secrets and deceptions. (978-1-63555-795-4)

Passion's Sweet Surrender by Ronica Black. Cam and Blake are unable to deny their passion for each other, but surrendering to love is a whole different matter. (978-1-63555-703-9)

The Holiday Detour by Jane Kolven. It will take everything going wrong to make Dana and Charlie see how right they are for each other. (978-1-63555-720-6)